# THE FORMS OF THINGS UNKNOWN

# The Forms of Things Unknown

## Short Stories by Maggie McNeill

-----------------First Edition, April 2017-----------------

Most of the stories within previously appeared in *The Honest Courtesan* (http://maggiemcneill.wordpress.com/) on the following dates: "Serpentine" (December 15th, 2014); "Left Behind" (January 15th, 2015); "Magna Mater" (February 12th, 2015); "What Gets Into a Man…?" (April 7th, 2012); "Shamhat" (May 15th, 2014); "Parallel Lines" (September 24th, 2012); "Tick Tock" (March 16th, 2015); "Millennium" (January 15th, 2014); "The Blessing" (November 14th, 2014); "Invasion" (February 13th, 2014); "Point of View" (February 15th, 2013); "Athena" (October 19th, 2015); "Eurydice" (July 16th, 2014); "Greek God" (September 12th, 2010); "Windows of the Soul" (March 18th, 2016); "Coming Up Short" (August 15th, 2014); "Split Focus" (May 15th, 2015); "Proxy" (January 18th, 2016); "The Reason for the Season" (December 16th, 2013); "Nothing Ventured" (May 16th, 2016); "Surprise" (April 17th, 2015); "Boss Lady" (November 16th, 2015); "Double X" (April 15th, 2014); "The Sum of Its Parts" (September 15th & 16th, 2014); "The Company of Strangers" (October 15th, 2014); "Heat" (August 17th, 2015); "Willpower" (July 17th, 2015); "Knock Knock Knock" (April 18th, 2016); "Little Girl Found" (September 21st, 2015); "Christmas Cookie" (December 18th, 2015); "Wise To Resolve" (June 16th, 2014); "The Generation of Leaves" (June 15th, 2015); "None of Woman Born" (June 17th, 2016); and "Travelers' Tales" (March 14th, 2014). "Eight Minute Warning" was written in 1993 but has not previously appeared in print, and "Trust Exercise" is new for this collection.

First Edition, April 2017
ISBN 1-541065-18-2
Printed in the United States of America
http://maggiemcneill.wordpress.com/

For Jae, now and always

# Table of Contents

## The Forms of Things Unknown

# Foreword

When I wrote the foreword for *Ladies of the Night*, I had no idea that my life was about to change dramatically from the way I'd been living it for years. At that time, I was still officially retired (though I'd been secretly working part-time under a different stage name since 2010) and my husband and I were still working to resolve the issues which had led to our estrangement (another issue I felt it best not to discuss in public). But by the time my book tour ended in Seattle in November, 2014, my husband and I had decided to divorce and I had decided to relocate to Seattle. Part of the reason for the relocation was the necessity of returning to work full-time post-divorce; part was the amazing community of sex workers which had welcomed me there with open arms and red-carpet treatment; and part was that I had been drawn into a whirlwind romance with a charming and fiery redheaded sex worker named Jae.

The changes in my lifestyle which accompanied my move also affected my writing; I had gone from a quiet and somewhat reclusive rural life on my ranch in Oklahoma, seeing only the occasional client and taking as much time to write as I wanted, to a hectic and very social urban life in the largest city I've ever lived in, working full-time and participating in a very intense lesbian relationship while still trying to get a column out every day. So it would be very surprising had my stories not changed as well, especially after Jae suffered a near-fatal motorcycle accident in August of 2015, which resulted in her hospitalization with grave injuries for two months. The abrupt shift from lover to caregiver was one of the most stressful experiences of my life, and it shows in my writing; though these stories aren't

## The Forms of Things Unknown

arranged chronologically I think the perceptive reader will be able to tell which were written before the move to Seattle, which after the move but before the accident, and which since the accident (which itself appears in fictionalized form in "Little Girl Found").

One of the big differences you will probably notice is that fewer than half of these stories contain a sex work element, compared to nearly all of the tales in *Ladies of the Night*; part of that is because I intentionally excluded several stories without whore characters from the first collection, and I think the expansion of my experiences also led to an expansion of my palette, so to speak. But perhaps the most important reason for the change is my being so totally out as a sex worker now. I've done so many TV and video interviews, and my picture has appeared so often on the internet, that strangers occasionally recognize me in public; many more people than that know my name and what I'm about. One of the reasons I published *Ladies* was to present whore-characters as people rather than cardboard props, but now that I'm doing that every publicly-spent hour of my life I reckon my Muse doesn't think it's *quite* so pressing anymore to have a harlot in every tale.

The unifying factor in this collection, as the title indicates, is things, situations or characters that aren't quite what they seem. Sometimes that's relatively benign, though more often (as you may already know if you're a long-time reader) it isn't. And in some cases, it's the story *itself* which isn't quite what it seems. There are several tales in which I and/or friends of mine appear in disguised, fictionalized forms, and two in which I *overtly* appear as a character; there are even a few places in which the boundaries between fiction and nonfiction, between story and introduction, and even between the confines of the book and the world outside

# *Foreword*

of its pages are deliberately blurred.  And when form and substance, fantasy and reality, creator and created are so fluid, anything can happen; I can't even guarantee that you, my readers, will remain firmly outside of the magic I've woven. After all, when real people can become characters and characters can emerge from the page to interact with their creator, how can the reader be sure to remain unaffected?  I hope that effect is limited to provoking your imagination and perhaps giving you a nightmare or two, but I'm not promising anything.

Don't say you weren't warned.

# The Forms of Things Unknown

*This story didn't yet exist when I started compiling this collection; I knew I wanted a new story for the first slot, but as I worked on editing the others, writing introductions, and doing the foreword, inspiration seemed reticent to show up. Finally, late one evening this title popped into my head, and within a few minutes I had the general outline of the story ...and realized it had been developing in the dark recesses of my brain for almost a year, sending out tendrils which turned into other tales before it was ready to come forth itself. The final spark, I think, came from several* Doctor Who *episodes I had watched recently, but the theme, imagery and substance are wholly native to my own psyche.*

# Trust Exercise

The door flew open without warning, but the child only barely flinched; her mother had been doing that quite often over the past few months, and she'd grown used to it as those too young to have any control over their environment are sometimes forced to. "Danielle, who were you talking to just now?"

"Nobody, Mommy."

"Don't tell me 'nobody', I heard you."

The deep brown eyes looked calmly up at her, and the little voice patiently explained, "Nobody real, Mommy. Just Barbie." She held up the doll, dressed incongruously in an evening gown, as if to illustrate the truth of her statement.

"You were *not* talking to Barbie!"

"But Mommy, who *else* would I be talking to?" she asked sagely. "There's nobody else here."

Anyone could have seen the child was telling the truth; the room contained neither window nor phone, the closet door was open, and the underside of the bed was occupied by drawers. Even if another child had somehow slipped into the apartment without Erica seeing, where would she be hiding? Besides, it had not sounded like Danielle was speaking to another child, but rather responding to an adult.

"I don't know what you're up to…"

"But Mommy, I'm not up…"

"SHUT UP! You're not to close this door any more, do you understand?"

"Yes, Mommy." She stood there staring for a few minutes as though unsure of what else to say, and then stormed off as quickly as she had appeared.

# The Forms of Things Unknown

By the time Danielle was four, she had realized that she was the only one who could see her strange visitors, and it didn't take many uncomfortable incidents to teach her that adults never reacted well to her conversations with them. The most benign response she could expect was some loud, mocking comment about her "imaginary friends"; others talked about her in hushed tones while sending worried glances in her direction; her Daddy seemed to think he should immediately interrupt and monopolize her attention for a while; and her kindergarten teacher insisted on lecturing her about the "proper time for make-believe" every time she caught her answering one of the visitors' all-too-frequent questions. Had it been up to Dani, she would've saved the visits for times when no other humans were around; unfortunately, it wasn't up to her. In their way, the visitors were just as rude and unreasonable as the adults in her life were; they might appear at any time of the day or night, seemingly oblivious to her circumstances or the presence of others, and would generally pepper her with all sorts of incomprehensible questions. Though she did her best to answer, she rarely even understood what was being asked; at first she reckoned the best solution to that was to ask a nearby adult for the meaning of any unknown words, but after unpleasant reactions ranging from laughter to slaps and scolding, she decided it was better to just figure it out on her own (a course of action eventually simplified by her discovery of the dictionary).

For a while, she tried simply ignoring the visitors when there were other people around, but that was even worse than talking to them; their usual response to her silence was to keep repeating the initial question more loudly and excitedly, and if she still ignored them they became

# *Trust Exercise*

increasingly upset and repeatedly asked her if she were OK until she finally responded. It all seemed quite absurd; couldn't they see her situation for themselves? It's true that they had no visible eyes, but then they had no visible features of *any* kind, and that didn't stop them from speaking and hearing. They appeared to her as lightless black humanoid forms, essentially three-dimensional shadows; like shadows their size and exact shape varied from one manifestation to another, and might even shift during the course of a visit. Eventually, she reasoned that they must see her as a black shape as well, which accounted for their seeming ignorance of her condition at any given time; after all, darkness impairs only vision, not speech. Usually only one of them appeared at a time, but there could be as many as three; she eventually learned to distinguish them from one another by voice and manner. Some visited her far more often than others, and as the years went by their numbers dwindled until nearly every visit was from the same individual, a patient and reassuring presence who said her name was Zoe. With familiarity came trust, and by the time Dani was nine they had worked out a signal by which she could let Zoe know when it wasn't a good time to talk.

"So who is Zoe?"

"Why, I'm surprised at you, Doctor Lang; she's my imaginary friend. You know that."

"That would've barely been an acceptable answer when you were ten, much less fourteen."

"OK, then, let's call her my spirit guide. Is that a more palatable response?"

9

# The Forms of Things Unknown

"I'm not your enemy, Dani. I'm trying to help you."

"Oh, please. You're trying to earn a living, same as everybody else. You wouldn't give a damn about me if my dad's insurance weren't reimbursing you."

"It's true that helping professionals need to earn a living just like everyone else, but that doesn't mean I don't genuinely care. You might think of my income as a subsidy which allows me to do the work I find rewarding, which is helping young people with their difficulties."

Dani rolled her darkly-lined eyes and sighed theatrically. "And you'll still kick me out at the 50-minute mark."

"Good job trying to make this about me. Look, I understand why you're upset; your mom had no right to read your diary, and if I were in your place I'd be angry too. She didn't tell me she was going to do it, and I would've discouraged her from doing it if she had. And I really am on your side, so if you'd rather not talk about Zoe we don't have to."

"I'd rather not. Let's just call her my Jungian shadow and leave it at that, OK?"

"Fair enough. Do you want to talk about how your mother's violating your privacy made you feel instead?"

And so they did, and many other topics over the next couple of years. But Zoe never came up again, because Danielle had learned it was absolutely *never* a good idea to mention anything about her to anyone else, no matter what their age and relationship to her. As she had aged the visits had become less frequent but longer, and more likely to occur when she was alone; she was also much better able to answer her shadowy visitor's questions, and she began to understand that the reason for her confusion in the past was that Zoe and the others had never adapted their questioning to a child's

10

# *Trust Exercise*

intellectual level, almost as though they hadn't understood that she *was* a child. But as that aspect of their interaction grew steadily less frustrating, another grew steadily more so: Zoe absolutely refused to discuss anything about herself and the others, or to answer any of Dani's questions. All she ever said in reply was, "I'm afraid you'll just have to trust me."

As the years went by, Erica slowly grew used to her daughter's strangeness; Danielle had learned to hide the more obvious signs, and draped the rest in the black lace and stylized manners of the Goth subculture. As Dani had calculated she would, Erica began to write off her weird ways as affected Goth behavior and adolescent rebelliousness, and when she got a scholarship to a prestigious art school her mother retroactively explained everything as the early signs of an artistic temperament. Eventually, her lesbianism became a bigger bone of contention than her "acting like a refugee from an Anne Rice novel" (as her father put it), and by the turn of the century they'd gotten over that as well, partly due to changes in the culture and partly because Dani was starting to make a very comfortable living from her *outre* artwork for the covers of horror novels and heavy metal CDs. By the time she turned thirty she caught less grief from them than she did from pouty girlfriends offended by her insistence upon living alone, but she had learned that lesson in the first third of her life: when Zoe came calling, she didn't want anyone else around to hear the conversation. Though these days, "argument" was probably a better word; now that she could be alone as much as she wanted to, Zoe didn't come around nearly as often. And

# The Forms of Things Unknown

when she did, she still totally avoided any discussion of her nature, knowledge or motives, responding instead with the now-familiar plea that Dani trust her.

It went on like that for most of her thirties; she painted, experimented with psychedelics, enjoyed casual sex, listened to music and read a great deal. Her work brought in a steady enough income and a steady stream of short-term girlfriends; if it weren't for shows and other professional contacts she'd have had barely any social life at all, because she had learned at an early age not to share too much with others. Zoe's visits had decreased to a few times a year, and she remained as unwilling as ever to discuss herself; Dani read widely on occult subjects, both in books and on the internet, but never found anything that seemed to put her on the right track for explaining what her strange, lifelong companion might be. Oh, there was plenty about spirit guides and familiars and guardian angels and tulpas and the like, but nothing that seemed quite the same as Zoe and her fellows. But though the research didn't give her what she was really looking for, it did help her in other ways; for one thing, it inspired her art, and that produced both practical and emotional rewards. It also made her sensitive to phenomena that she had never noticed before.

At first it was little things: flashes of precognition or clairvoyance. Strings of odd coincidences. Objects turning up in places she hadn't put them. People claiming that events had happened a little differently from the way she recalled them. Weird computer glitches. Then slowly, over a period of years, they grew gradually worse and more frequent: memory lapses. Paintings in progress having hours of work added while she was asleep, or some of the colors changing. Small objects disappearing, appearing or changing into other things. The city demanding payment for parking tickets

# *Trust Exercise*

when she didn't even own a car, then denying they'd sent the letter. Appliances burning out. The balance in her bank account fluctuating from day to day.

And then Zoe started visiting a lot more often again. And Dani decided it was time for some answers.

One grey December afternoon she returned from the grocery to find that virtually none of the things she had purchased were in her shopping bag. The apples had become oranges; the sirloin had been replaced with pork chops; the deodorant had somehow transformed into three packages of light bulbs; the potato chips had reverted into raw potatoes; the cinnamon had been switched for a jar of mayonnaise (and she *hated* mayonnaise). And while the yogurt was still yogurt, it was of a brand she had never even *heard* of before, much less bought. As she stood there dumbfounded, she realized Zoe was across the kitchen island from her.

"Are you going to tell me what's going on, or just tell me to trust you for the thousandth time?"

"Danielle, I don't actually know what's going on. Or rather, I *do* know, but I don't know what it looks like to you."

"What's *that* supposed to mean?"

"I know that what you perceive as reality is in flux, and it's probably beginning to get creepy. But I don't know what that actually looks like to you. Would you mind telling me?"

"Oh, I can give you an exact *catalog* of what it looks like!" she snapped, turning to pick up a steno book from the counter, and then reading off a long list of odd happenings, complete with dates and times, and ending with today's grocery incident. "And that's just the past two years; it was going on for some time before I finally decided to start logging it."

Zoe had listened patiently to the long, long list, and when Dani was done she said, "I have some good news and some bad news for you."

"The good news being?"

"This will all be over in a relatively short time."

"And the bad news?"

"It's going to get a lot worse before that."

Danielle had never been a crier; she was always too afraid of how others might react to her truth, so she expressed her emotions on canvas. But this was too much; she broke down and started weeping, not in fear or sorrow but in anger. "What is this all about? And why is it happening to me?"

"Because you don't belong here."

"What's that supposed to mean?"

"Just what I said. You don't belong in this world; you belong in mine. That's why only you can see and hear us, Dani; you aren't one of these beings. You're one of us."

"A black shapeshifting shadow thing?"

"No. Actually, that's what you look like right now to me, too. It's just that your senses can't properly interpret conditions on my side of the veil, and vice-versa."

"So how did I get here?"

"It was an accident."

"*An accident*? Are you fucking kidding me? All this was a goddamned accident?"

"And how is that different from anyone else's life? A great deal of what goes on in the universe is due to random chance; sometimes the accidents are fortunate, and sometimes unfortunate. This is a bit of both."

"So why couldn't you tell me this before? And why tell me now?"

## Trust Exercise

"Because your situation here is very delicate. As I said, you don't belong here, but we don't have the power to just reach in and pull you out; we need to wait until you 'come out of the other side of the pipe', as it were. And that time is coming. Your being here is a violation of the natural order of things, and this continuum is starting to reject you."

"Like an allergic reaction?"

"Something like that. This incarnation is beginning to disintegrate, and when it does we'll be ready to pull you out."

"So why can't you just do it now?"

"Because the forces of reality are still too strong right now; if we tried we'd rip you to shreds."

There was a long silence, finally broken by Dani. "And why couldn't you tell me all this before?"

"Because if you had known, you might have tried to leave this incarnation by brute force."

"In other words, kill myself."

"Right. And if you had, you'd have been lost to us forever. We couldn't risk it."

"I thought about it lots of times, you know."

"Why do you think we got so frantic whenever you wouldn't answer us? Until we learned how you would react while in that body, we had to keep you under nearly-constant supervision. Or as constant as the timelines allow."

"Time moves differently for you than for me?"

"Yes."

"Slower for me, of course."

"Unfortunately, yes."

"Like fairyland."

"Excuse me?"

## *The Forms of Things Unknown*

"There's a human legend that there are other beings living alongside humans, and if a person stumbles into their world and stays what he thinks is a few hours or overnight, he might return home to find decades or even centuries had passed."

"There's often a grain of truth in legends. Sometimes more than just a grain."

Dani sighed and ran her fingers through her hair. "So what do you need me to do now?"

"I think you already know the answer."

"Trust you."

"I'm afraid so. It won't be much longer now. A few years at most."

"A few *years*?"

"I'm sorry, Dani. I'm sure it must be agonizing for you, but there's no other way. On this side, it's going to be so soon we're already scrambling to be ready."

She nodded. "I get it." And then, more softly: "Zoe?"

"Yes?"

"When I'm safely on your side, will I be able to touch you?"

"Yes, dear, absolutely. As much and as often as you want to."


For a while, Dani found comfort in Zoe's words, but then she began to outsmart herself. Children, especially unhappy or maltreated children, often fantasize that they're adopted and their "real" parents would someday come and rescue them; how was this different? What if this was simply the manifestation of some deep narcissism, a belief that she must be "better" than other people, a magical princess lost in

16

# *Trust Exercise*

a barbarian land?  But Zoe hadn't claimed their people were "better" or "higher", just different, and if this were a delusion, it was a remarkably persistent one:  four decades without substantially altering until recently.  Even if she felt she couldn't trust her memories, there were the journals; she'd been keeping them since she was about 12, and Zoe was in them over and over from the beginning.  No, she had no choice but to believe what her guardian – as she now recognized Zoe to be – told her.  If it were false and she believed it, how was that different from the rest of her life?  But if it were true and she *dis*believed it…what was it Zoe had said?  *"You'd have been lost to us forever."*  Not worth the risk.

And so she persevered while things grew steadily worse.  Names of people and things changed back and forth.  She'd go to bed with a slender redhead and wake up next to a busty brunette, or on one notable occasion a man.  One day she came home to find an aquarium full of tropical fish; the next morning it had become two gerbils in a cage, and a few days later it was a miniature schnauzer for a few hours before turning into a one-eyed Himalayan cat which soon vanished while she was out of town, litterbox and all.  She might go for hours without being able to read anything because it was all written in some strange foreign tongue using an alphabet she'd never seen.  The date began to change unexpectedly, then the season, and she seemed to have skipped the majority of 2015 because mid-February was followed by late October, with no memory of anything in between and a number of bank deposits for artworks she couldn't remember painting.  Twice she woke up in different apartments, and then the

## The Forms of Things Unknown

same apartment building moved overnight to a different city. And still Zoe asked her to be patient, and to trust.

After that lost year the changes became more rapid, radical and confusing; Dani had to stop taking recreational drugs entirely because she wanted to be absolutely sure that the phenomena she was experiencing were "real" and undistorted…and because she was afraid one substance might turn into a very different one without her noticing. She had come this far without checking out, and now that she was so close to the end she didn't want to risk doing so by accident. The only constants now were Zoe and herself; everything else was subject to unpredictable and increasingly-horrifying change. And then one day she noticed a different name on a piece of mail…and soon realized that same name was on every document she had. Even *she* was in flux now, and that had to be a sign of approaching the end. She was being rejected by this universe. It was forming a cyst around her, in preparation for expelling her entirely. She lost track of time as days and nights of wildly-variable length followed one another in no particular order, and the weather changed chaotically; there seemed no rhyme or reason to the date display on her shapeshifting cell phone. She found herself in places without knowing how she got there, doing things she could no longer understand, while the lights flickered and things changed color and the ground itself shifted under a sky that had torn open and was bleeding profusely. The people around her changed their shapes, and she could no longer tell them apart; they turned into three-dimensional shadows, but of a dingy grey rather than an impenetrable black. The buildings rotted, and the ground began to bubble, and the air reverberated with titanic cracking sounds that dwarfed thunder as that does the sound of an egg breaking. She began to scream as her own body began to melt, as objects began to disperse like powder in the wind, as the sky itself began to disintegrate.

"Dani. It's time."

In the center of her vision was a humanoid shape, a dingy grey shadow like all the others, but for two differences: it was stable while the others ran like water, and from it came the familiar voice of Zoe, the one unchanging factor across the entirety of her life. The one thing she absolutely *knew* she could trust, the one totally dependable chain connecting the shards of her existence. Zoe. I love you, Zoe.

"I love you too, Dani. Are you ready?"

"I'm afraid."

"I know, darling. Me too."

The ground had completely vanished from beneath Zoe, and Dani had the urge to run lest she fall into the abyss yawning before her.

"No."

"But the ground, I'll fall!"

"Let yourself."

"No!"

"You have to. Trust me, Dani. I'll catch you. Promise."

Dani was confused and terrified and wanted to flee, but...how could she not trust Zoe, after all this time? She surrendered to the force of gravity, and let herself fall headlong into the abyss.


She awoke in a quiet, peaceful place with gentle fingers stroking her head, but when she opened her eyes what she saw seemed a confused jumble of color. "Zoe?"

# The Forms of Things Unknown

"I'm here, love. Close your eyes, it's going to take you a while to adjust."

"But I'm safe?"

She could hear the smile in Zoe's voice, even though she couldn't see it. "Oh yes, dear one, you're safe at last!"

"I want to see what you look like!"

"Your mind doesn't yet know how to interpret the visual images in our world, but it won't take long to learn."

"How long?"

"I don't know, a few years maybe?"

"Years?" but then she heard Zoe's laughter and caught on: "Ah, you mean Earthly years; time passes more quickly here!"

"Yes. I hope you'll forgive the joke."

"I'd forgive you anything." She disobediently opened her eyes again, taking in as much of the jumble of shapes and colors as she could before she was forced to close them. "It's so bright and colorful here, colors I don't even have names for! I thought this world would be dark and eerie, like the worlds in my paintings."

"No, darling; this is your true world. Those pictures were how your soul perceived the world you were in. It's not that their world is so much worse than ours; it's just that you didn't belong, and could therefore never completely understand it or feel comfortable there. But now you're home, and while it's far from perfect it's where you belong."

"It's a bit frightening to think I have to start all over again, like a baby."

"Well, not quite a baby. But you are very young yet. You'll catch on quickly, and I'll be here to help you."

"I know you will. Who are you, Zoe? I mean, why do you care about me? Are you just a helping professional, like Dr. Lang? Or is it more than that?"

## *Trust Exercise*

"Well, things here aren't quite the same as in the world you're used to, but I think 'sister' is probably the closest approximation." Dani suddenly clung tightly to her, as though she were about to fall again. "Oh, sweet child, you needn't fret; I'm here and everything's going to be all right from now on. You can trust me on that."

Dani smiled and relaxed in Zoe's arms, because she knew at last with absolute certainty that she could.

# The Forms of Things Unknown

*Every December, I feature a different kind of story in my blog; they're usually light, and some contain puzzles. This one certainly isn't light, but it's...well, you'll see. It also contains a number of in-jokes and veiled references, and partakes of the ancient holiday custom of reversal: it treats as serious a topic I spend considerable time ridiculing. This really isn't as odd as it may at first appear; one of the defining characteristics of myths and legends is that they are interesting (which is why people tell and retell them). A dull myth would soon fade, and the human mind has a congenital preference for fascinating nonsense over dull fact...which, of course, explains the persistence of urban legends and moral panics no matter how often and thoroughly their elements are debunked. And as generations of science fiction and fantasy writers have discovered, this makes stuff like Atlantis, ancient astronauts, the hollow Earth, etc wonderful subjects for stories, even if the author doesn't actually believe a word of them. Keep that in mind when you read this tale, which is intentionally ambiguous: is what appears to be going on herein what is* actually *going on? Does our protagonist have a highly overactive imagination? Or is her antagonist just enjoying a cruel joke at her expense?*

# Serpentine

The doorman glowered at her as though he were the personification of the grim building itself, which had been the tallest one in town for over 30 years but was now humbled by the titans which had recently grown up around it. Jane imagined it must be indignant at this development, and that its frowning façade was silently telling her, *"Go away, you have no business here."* But if she was going to make it as a reporter, she could let neither unfriendly employees nor gloomy old buildings stop her…and besides, her coat was really much too thin for this weather, and it had begun to snow; she went up to the door and tried to ignore the unpleasant expression on its keeper's face.

Once within, she walked directly to the desk and announced that she was there to see Miss Morelli. "Do you have an appointment?" asked the attendant, in a tone of voice that seemed to add *"I know you don't."*

"No, but please tell her Miss Louis from the Archdiocese is here to ask for her support in providing Christmas dinners for the poor." It was a terrible lie, but Margo Morelli was known to be even more generous with Catholic charities than her late father had been; Jane hoped it would be enough.

The attendant sighed, "You don't have to talk to Miss Morelli herself about that; just see her personal assistant, Miss Angelo. Go on up to the eleventh floor," he said, gesturing toward the elevator with the phone receiver, "and I'll let her know you're on the way."

"God bless you!" said Jane, feeling even more ashamed about her deception. *"Still,"* she thought, *"a girl has to eat, and jobs are scarce these days. I'll just have to go*

# The Forms of Things Unknown

*to confession this weekend."* She involuntarily started at the ornate décor of the elevator doors, which seemed somehow menacing to her. But she only paused for a moment; it was too late to turn back now, and there was only one more obstacle between her and the interview she wanted. As she expected, the public elevator did not even *go* to the twelfth floor, so even if she had somehow been able to bribe the operator he could not have granted her request. Correction: she actually *was* going to the twelfth floor, though the number said eleven; the building was numbered in the European style, so that the first floor was the one above ground level. But the Italians consider thirteen a *lucky* number, don't they? So it made sense that the boss's office should be on that floor even if the number said twelve.

Miss Angelo turned out to be a tiny lady in late middle age with the hawk-like demeanor of a strict nun, and Jane felt her heart sink; there was no way she could even lie convincingly to this woman, much less prevail upon her to shirk her duty and let Jane through. So there was only one choice: the naked truth. "Miss Angelo, I feel terrible about having to tell a fib to get in here, but I'm desperate to talk to Miss Morelli. You see, I haven't got a job or any family in town, and my rent is long overdue, but I'm a good writer so I just *know* I can get a job as a reporter if I can get a scoop. Ever since Miss Morelli's father passed on she's been unwilling to talk to any reporters, but I thought maybe because she and I are both women trying to make it in businesses dominated by men, that she'd have pity on me." Jane's tears were real; she was desperate, and lacked even the money to wire her family out West for help.

Miss Angelo regarded her with a penetrating but not-unkind gaze for agonizingly-long moments, then directed her back into the waiting room with, "I'll see what I can do."

# Serpentine

Jane's heart was pounding, but the fact that she hadn't been instantly thrown out on her ear gave her some hope; she obediently returned to the anteroom and tried to calm herself. It was no use; she got more and more nervous, and when Miss Angelo suddenly appeared in the doorway Jane almost screamed. "Miss Morelli will see you. Come this way, and mind your manners."

She led Jane down a hall to what seemed the back of the building, where they entered an elevator that did indeed go all the way to twelve. But when the doors opened on the floor above, Jane was taken aback by what met her eyes. She had expected a well-lit outer office with a secretary who would usher her into the inner sanctum, but instead she found herself in a sort of vestibule opening to a large, luxuriously-appointed space only dimly lit by lamps, as one might illuminate a bedroom. She heard the doors close behind her, and Miss Angelo was gone; Jane was apparently all alone. Nervously, she crept forward into the vast office; the huge mahogany desk was topped with some kind of green, patterned stone, the walls behind the desk were lined with books, and the tall windows showed her that the snow flurry had become a storm. Though it was only mid-afternoon the gloom outside did little to alleviate the shadow within; most of the light was coming from another room to her right, and she gasped as she realized that there was a woman standing in that doorway watching her. She was breathtakingly beautiful, and the light streaming past her seemed to envelop her in a kind of aura which intensified the effect. But at the same time Jane was terrified, not just by her reputation but by something less definable.

## The Forms of Things Unknown

"Good afternoon, Miss Louis; I'm Margo Morelli. May I get you a drink?"

"A...a drink?" she asked stupidly. Jane's parents were teetotalers, and even after leaving home she had been too timid to risk breaking the law, even if anyone had invited her to a party (which nobody had anyway).

The older woman smiled warmly. "Yes. It's even legal again now, you know."

"Um...yes," stammered Jane. "Actually, that's what I came to talk to you about."

"Oh?" she asked, then "What will you have?"

"Uh, whatever you're having is fine." Jane couldn't tell Bourbon from Bordeaux or brandy from beer, so it hardly mattered. She accepted the much-too-large drink, and took a sip; its taste was strange and unpleasant to her, and she couldn't hide the face she made when she swallowed it. Her hostess pretended not to notice, and seated herself on the other side of the desk.

"So what can I do for you?"

"Well," Jane said, "with the passage of the 21$^{st}$ Amendment last week, Prohibition is over; that means it's legal to sell liquor again, which means your organization won't be making any money from, ah, irregular imports any more..."

"Well put, and exactly correct." If Miss Morelli was annoyed with the topic, she didn't show it.

"...so even though you have plenty of other business interests, both...ummm...regular and irregular, you stand to lose a lot of income. You don't strike me as the kind of woman who will take that lying down."

"Again, exactly correct." Still no sign of anger, but she wasn't helping either; Jane's vision had now fully adjusted to the dim lighting, and she could clearly see those

26

# *Serpentine*

deep black eyes fixed upon her in a way she did not like at all. She took another long sip, and despite the awful taste she had to admit it did seem to calm her nerves somewhat.

"So...what do you plan to do about it?"

Miss Morelli leaned back slightly in her chair and laughed, a genuine laugh in which Jane nonetheless thought she detected considerable menace. "You are a charmingly naïve little bird, do you realize that? It's why I agreed to see you. That, and the fact that both Miss Angelo and the downstairs attendant told me you were quite fetching. They were not wrong."

Jane felt herself blush furiously, and hoped the light was too dim for it to show. She took a gulp. "I...that is...um..."

"Listen, little bird. Surely you didn't think I'd be fool enough to go on the record answering such a ridiculous question? Until someone invents a recording device small enough to fit in a purse, nothing I tell you would be admissible in federal court; however, my father taught me never to stir up hornets' nests without reason. It's why our family has run this city since you were in pigtails. Had you been a professional reporter instead of a little girl playing at it, you'd never have been let through the front door."

Jane was so totally mortified she couldn't speak, but the lovely contralto continued. "Still, it amuses me to humor you, so I'll answer your question. Yes, I'm already planning to expand another of my 'irregular' businesses, as you so charmingly put it. Would you like me to tell you which one?" Perhaps it was because of the bird metaphor, but she now had the distinct mental image of her hostess as a beautiful serpent, holding her fascinated as it moved in for

## The Forms of Things Unknown

the kill.  Her head was gently spinning from the unfamiliar
effect of the liquor, and she felt unable to speak, let alone
flee.  "Have you ever heard of white slavery?"

"Oh, no," Jane said weakly.  "You wouldn't!"

"Does anyone know where you are right now?"

As if she had no control over it, her own mouth
betrayed her.  "No."  Her equally-traitorous body refused to
move as the other woman slid across the green stone desktop
and began to stroke her hair, and to her total horror
something deep inside her responded to the caress.  Finally,
she was able to regain enough self-control to drain the
tumbler and ask, "What if I refused to go quietly?  Would
you pull a gun on me, or call one of your thugs to manhandle
me?"

"Nothing so crude, I assure you."  The voice was
gentle now, almost reassuring, as she took the glass from
Jane's trembling fingers.

"What, then?" the girl asked, fighting a wave of
drowsiness that was slowly engulfing her.

"I'd simply drug your drink."

*Serpentine*

# The Forms of Things Unknown

*After writing "Serpentine", I conceived of the notion of making it the first of a loose trilogy, connected not by characters, events or setting, but by several shared motifs and in-jokes (one obvious, the others less so). This is the second in that trilogy, and as you'll see the main motif is much more literal herein; the last one, which is next in this collection, takes the whole thing to its logical conclusion.*

# Left Behind

Jacob Ellis was a nervous young man. That is, he was *habitually* nervous; he had trouble sitting still for long unless he occupied his hands with something, and it was often difficult for him to focus on the task before him unless he was very, very interested in it. It wasn't that he was stupid; quite the opposite in fact. His mind was so agile, so filled with curiosity, that he found it difficult to keep it from wandering to things that were more worthy of consideration than the dull matters of clerking. But since it had been determined long ago that he would follow his father into the legal profession, that was what he had done, despite the fact that he would probably have been more suited to a trade involving more motion and less focus on dry-as-dust wills, deeds, contracts and all the other mundane matters of a family law practice.

But today, he was also *situationally* nervous, because his father had entrusted him with his first important client: the estate of Magnolia Machen, the wealthiest woman in the county. Mr. Machen had been killed in the War, and since many a lost fortune and devastated farm had been left behind in General Sherman's wake, it had not been difficult for his widow to purchase a grand old house (in need of some repair) and most of the other valuable land in the area, and to build up a considerable income from it. And since Mrs. Machen was a woman of reclusive and frugal ways, that income had enabled her to invest in the stock market and to acquire other, more valuable properties stretching from coast to coast.

She was so reclusive, in fact, that Jake had not even been aware that she had a daughter until his father told him that he was to meet her at the house today. And that meeting

# The Forms of Things Unknown

was the cause of yet a third layer of nervousness: Miss Machen was stunningly beautiful, with mounds of lustrous hair, dark, piercing eyes and a sinuous grace that more befit a dancer than a debutante. Being in her presence filled him with powerful feelings he could not clearly define and was not at all comfortable with, and he felt himself perspiring under his seersucker to a degree he felt was profuse, even considering the June heat. Could she really be almost forty years old? She didn't look a day over twenty-two, but if she were that young she'd have been born more than ten years after the late Mr. Machen's demise. Best not to think too hard about it. "You'll have to forgive me, Miss, but up until today I wasn't even aware that you existed; I had assumed the estate would go to more distant relatives."

If she noticed his clumsy handling of the statement, she was far too well-mannered to show it. "I haven't lived here since before you were born. You see, my mother was a singularly cold-blooded woman, and didn't really want to be burdened with a child. So I was shipped off at a very young age to be educated in Europe, and have lived with various relatives in various parts of three continents since then. I have only seen my mother a handful of times since childhood, and the only reason I was here when she died was that she wrote me a letter summoning me here a few weeks ago, once her doctor told her that she only had a little while yet to live."

"I'm sorry for your loss," said Jake, mostly because he couldn't think of anything else to say. He was a bit surprised that Doc Thompson's prognosis had been so accurate; he had been largely retired for twenty years, and the only people who still consulted him were those more concerned with his legendary discretion than with his very average level of skill. Thompson probably knew about the

# *Left Behind*

dirty laundry and closet skeletons of most of the best families in the region, and would take that knowledge to the grave in a very few years. It had been a very profitable specialization for him; people said there was no secret, however dark, that a sufficient sum could not persuade him to keep.

Miss Machen shrugged. "Hardly a loss, Mr. Ellis; as I just told you, she and I weren't very close. The only reason her death affects me more than the death of a business associate is that it stands to be extremely profitable for me."

Even after hearing about their estrangement, Miss Machen's coldness in regard to her mother shocked him. *I reckon the apple didn't fall far from the tree*, he thought; *I won't be surprised to hear she sends her daughter away, too.* But out loud he said, "Well, um, yes…that is, ah, er, you're her sole beneficiary."

"I'm well aware of the contents of the will, Mr. Ellis; my mother did not like surprises, and was therefore not one to inflict them on others." Her voice was soft as silk, but her gaze sank into his being like…he preferred not to think about it. "In fact, if it's all the same to you we can dispense with the customary formalities; I'd rather just sign what I have to sign and then be on my way. I've a train to New Orleans to catch in only a few hours."

"Of course; my father has been your mother's attorney since the early seventies, so it's the least I can do to, ah, expedite things for you. There are just, um, a few questions…"

"Oh?" The brief syllable dripped impatience.

"Um, yes, well, just one really important one, and a minor one. First, I see we have a copy of the death certificate, but there's absolutely nothing anywhere about funeral arrangements."

"My mother didn't believe in such frivolities, nor do I. Her remains were cremated."

"C-c-c-cremated?"

"You find that frightening?" The trace of a smile flickered across the lovely lips, but only for an instant.

"N-no, not exactly, it's just, um, I've never seen that done before."

"There are no local crematories, Mr. Ellis; my mother's doctor took the body to the nearest one. It's all in these papers, and the ashes are in that urn." She gestured to a rather plain metal container placed unceremoniously among other boxes on the parlor table. "Now what was the other matter?"

"Oh, um, it's just these, um, Arizona ranch holdings; I don't have all the information I need to deal with them from here, and I'd rather not have to bill you for a trip all the way out there."

"I believe a telegram to my attorney in Denver would clear that up," she said, rising from her seat; "I'll just tell him to respond directly to you."

Since Miss Machen had pointed it out, Jake had been unable to keep his mind off of the urn; he had never seen the ashes of a human body before, and was consumed with curiosity about what they would be like. Were they fine, or coarse? Were the teeth and bones wholly reduced, or were there still shards? He just had to see, and Miss Machen would be on the telephone with the telegraph office for at least a few minutes. What would be the harm? After all, neither the old lady nor her daughter seemed very sentimental about the remains, and neither of them was in a position to see him peeking anyhow. He turned to the container and

# Left Behind

lifted the lid, but was startled and confused when he found
not ashes, but something white and papery. He quickly
glanced down the hall to be sure his hostess was not yet
returning, then reached into the jar and pulled out the
contents. As a boy he had once seen the cast-off skin of a
snake, thin and translucent but still retaining the shape of the
animal which had left it behind when it became too old and
worn to be of use any longer; that's what the thing in the urn
reminded him of, though it was much larger. And though
it had been crumpled and broken in the process of
compressing it into the undersized container, it was still quite
obvious that the creature which had shed this decrepit husk
was possessed of a human shape.

# The Forms of Things Unknown

*This is the last part of the loose trilogy which started with "Serpentine" and continued with "Left Behind". As I explained in the latter preface, they are not connected by characters, events or setting, but by shared motifs. Some of those motifs are closer to the surface in this offering, while others are hidden much more deeply; one of those is the erotic undertone, which most of you probably wouldn't even have noticed had I not said something. The title is of course Latin, and means "Great Mother"; it was the name under which the Anatolian mother goddess Cybele was worshipped in Rome. In early times these rituals were rather bloody and not at all nice, including castration of a male sacrifice who thus represented Cybele's lover Attis (the later myth of Aphrodite and Adonis descended from it). By the second century CE a bull had replaced the human, but the attending sacred drama was still a great deal darker and earthier than most Romans were comfortable with; the cult has therefore provided material to generations of horror writers.*

# Magna Mater

Guthrie, Oklahoma Territory
February 12<sup>th</sup>, 1895

For almost thirty-five years you have been
wonderfully patient with me, dear sister; you have respected
my wish not to talk about the events of that fateful trip of my
youth in which my first husband met his maker. For all that
time I have allowed both you and the authorities to believe
that hostile Indians were to blame, and that the nervous shock
was so great I was unable to discuss the details. Now, I don't
give a damn if the law continues to abide in ignorance about
it, but a decent respect for my own kin and for the kindness
you showed me after my return, going far beyond what I had
any right to expect from you, demands that I take this
opportunity to break my silence at last and tell you the truth
about what happened, why it happened and why I have never
said anything about it. I leave it to your discretion as to how
much (if any) you wish to share with Richard and Janice;
perhaps it would be better for you to invent something
instead. You always were the imaginative one; I could never
come up with tales like you could, which is why I never even
tried to make up some fib to cover up the truth. I ask you to
remember that when reading this; I tell it exactly as it
happened, and you well know that I could never have
dreamed anything like this up. As to my children…well,
Richard is a good, simple man like his father was, and would
certainly conclude that his mother was mad and had run off
into the hinterlands in some kind of fit. But Janice is my
daughter for sure, and may eventually need to know (as you
will see).

# The Forms of Things Unknown

I don't recall the exact date when we left Shreveport, but it was sometime in the spring of 1860; I want to say April, but it's so warm down in Louisiana it may have actually been earlier. We sailed up the Red River until we reached the western part of what was then called the Indian Territory, and is now known as Oklahoma; after we disembarked we were taken by a guide back into the hills. As you may recall, George was in search of evidence to support his theories about the spread of myth-motifs, and he had received reports that the Indians who had inhabited this area prior to the mass relocations of the thirties had worshipped a goddess similar to the Aztec Cihuacoatl (that means "Snake Woman"). For two years he had sent letters back and forth to academics, naturalists, explorers, military officers, government officials and anyone else he thought might have some information on the area, and by the autumn of '59 he had enough to convince his dean to grant him a sabbatical for field research. The amount of money Miskatonic granted him, however, was not enough to both pay for the trip and hire an assistant; he therefore hit upon the practical solution of marrying a Mount Holyoke graduate who had planned to become a missionary to the Indians anyway, and not bothering to tell her that his mission to the Southwest was to *study* the heathens rather than converting them. Don't think too badly of him, dear sister; though it is true he married a young and naïve girl to gain an unpaid servant and secretary, it is equally true that I married a middle-aged professor to gain financial support and social status. Does that shock you? It shouldn't; after all, in those days even pursuing an education was a rather unconventional choice for a woman.

I won't bore you with all the details of the time we spent following fruitless leads, interviewing old Indians with

# *Magna Mater*

the help of translators, investigating sites that were said to have been sacred to now-extinct tribes, and otherwise chasing wild geese. George grew increasingly desperate (and increasingly irritable) as summer turned to autumn without our having discovered even enough to base an article on. He began to follow ever-weaker clues to ever-more-distant destinations, and as the money ran low he eschewed the use of guides entirely; it is therefore unsurprising that late in October we found ourselves quite lost in a desolate region that showed no signs of recent habitation by either white men or red, taking shelter from a torrential downpour in a low cave which we had discovered only that very morning. After we had been there several hours and eaten the last of the provisions we had brought from the nearest trading post several days earlier, George began to fret terribly; had there been room enough I'm sure he would have paced, but in the circumstances he lacked even that meager outlet for his nervous energy. But as he became ever more agitated, I became correspondingly calmer; somehow I *knew* we would be all right, because we were being watched over by an angel. Finally I told George as much, and…well, I can't repeat the things he shouted at me. Stung by his mistreatment I retreated more deeply into the cave, where I discovered a heretofore-unnoticed bend that, after a short tunnel that had to be traversed on hands and knees, opened up into a large, high-ceilinged cavern dimly illuminated through some fissure above by what little daylight there was. And in that space I saw the unmistakable signs of intelligent habitation.

Returning to the front I called my husband, and though he at first ignored my entreaties his curiosity

## The Forms of Things Unknown

eventually got the better of him. When he entered the room he visibly brightened a little, then became more excited about the artifacts I had found, which he said resembled none he had seen yet that year. He also remarked that everything seemed extremely worn, as though it had been used regularly for a very, very long time. And while he investigated further, handling object after object, I became aware of the distinct feeling of being watched. George did not seem to notice, and dismissed my impressions until we both heard the soft scraping sound of something heavy being dragged across the bare stone floor. We then whirled together, and were confronted with the occupant of this hidden abode.

She was a being who had seemingly come forth out of the realm of legend; from the waist up she was a beautiful, ageless woman with a huge mane of thick, somewhat stiff hair, but below the waist she was a gigantic serpent whose skin bore a complex pattern. I'm sure you think this apparition must have been utterly horrifying, but I assure you she was quite the opposite; in fact, she was absolutely the most magnificent creature I have ever seen, and I felt as safe in her presence as I would have in our mother's arms. *Do not be afraid,* she seemed to say to me, though her mouth never moved; *my kind are friends and benefactors to humanity, and have long watched over you. I know that you and your mate are lost, and I will draw you a map so that you may find your way back to human places tomorrow morning.*

But as I listened, I slowly became aware of another sound, that of George's raised voice. And I suddenly realized he was pointing a shotgun at our hostess; he probably would have already fired had I not been so close to her. "For God's sake, Tillie, step back!" he shouted; "This monster has mesmerized you, like a snake fascinates a bird!"

40

## *Magna Mater*

"What nonsense, George!" I said matter-of-factly; "Don't you know who this is? It's the very goddess you have been looking for all these months! This is Cihuacoatl, the Snake Woman, and she and her kind have watched over humanity since we were driven out of Eden!"

"Listen to yourself!" he screamed in near-terror; "Is this any way for a seminary graduate to talk? It's a devil who has bewitched your mind!"

"A devil?" I asked, confused. "She is as beautiful as an angel!"

"Why do you keep calling this monster 'she'? Tillie, please come away before it strikes!"

But it was too late. George had turned his attention to me, and away from the Lady; I have never seen any living thing move so quickly. In an instant she was upon him; the gun was hurled against the far wall, and in only a few more seconds he was surrounded by her coils. He struggled for a while, then grew still, and as he expired in her embrace she wept - not soft crocodile tears, but great racking sobs of true anguish. By contrast, I merely stood mutely and watched him die, nor did I feel any but the smallest twinge when she released his lifeless form to collapse on the floor. *I am truly sorry, my daughter.*

"I don't understand why he reacted so; it was as though he couldn't see or hear you as I do."

*He couldn't.* Her exquisite shoulders slumped, and she sighed audibly. *It has ever been so. Though we have guided and protected your race since before you had the power of speech, a certain fraction of your people are deaf to the means by which we communicate...and they invariably react to the sight of us with terror.* We talked long into the

41

# The Forms of Things Unknown

night, as though the corpse of my husband was not lying in the next room; she explained that hers was an ancient race from a day when the Earth was warmer and wetter; they were extremely long-lived but neither numerous nor fertile, and had long ago adopted humanity as their heirs. They appeared in the myths of many countries as the nagas of India, the dragons of China, the feathered serpent of Mexico, and other benevolent creatures; but because of those who were blind to their beauty they also inspired legends of fearsome creatures like the lamia of European legend and the serpent of Genesis. Perhaps you may agree that she was a demon, and that she made me one by association; perhaps you feel as though she could have stopped George without killing him. But you have neither seen her nor heard her voice, and George was ready and able to murder an ancient, benevolent creature, perhaps the last of her kind, for no reason other than his own animal fear; had she released him, he would have organized a monster hunt within hours.

The next day I followed her directions and returned to the trading post alone; my serenity and lack of concern were interpreted as symptoms of shock, and the traders were so ready to believe that George had been killed by hostile Comanches that I didn't even have to make up a lie. I was still quiet and contemplative when I returned to Massachusetts, and everyone (including you) made the same assumption as the traders had. Eventually I remarried and had children, so everyone assumed I had "recovered". But I was never the same; for all these years and across half a continent I have never been out of contact with My Lady, and many a time I have sat in my house in the still of night, hearing her whisper to me across many hundreds of miles. She has given me advice, comfort and solace as needed, and because of her I have never felt alone. But now my husband

## Magna Mater

is dead and my children are grown, and I am no longer needed here; and the Great Mother is old and in sore need of my company and assistance, though she will yet survive me by centuries. So I must go to her, to faithfully serve her as she has served our whole race. And know this, dear sister: though you and others may think me mad, I have never been saner or happier.

> With All My Love,
> I Remain Very Truly Yours,
>
> Tillie

.

*(With grateful acknowledgement to the works of A. Merritt and H.P. Lovecraft).*

# The Forms of Things Unknown

*Several of the stories in this collection were written before I started doing my blog, and this is one of them. I wrote it on March 30th, 1997 (Easter Sunday that year), about six months before I started stripping; it actually came to me in a dream, and I woke up and typed it out before breakfast. The heroine isn't a sex worker of any kind, and neither is she me; though I experienced the dream in first person and her brother was "played" by my own brother, she's a great deal more submissive both to family and convention than I ever was. As you may have noticed from stories like "Pandora" in* Ladies of the Night, *many of my most memorable dreams are vaguely unsettling; this one is no exception.*

# What Gets Into a Man...?

On Easter Sunday my brother called me to ask if I wanted to go to church. I had not actually planned to, but in the face of his request I decided to genuflect to convention and attend Easter mass with him. By the time I had gotten dressed and made up it was rather late, and we just barely made the last mass of the morning, the high mass, which had actually already started when we arrived. The church was absolutely jammed as churches are only on Easter, and as we arrived late we were forced to stand in the aisle near the front doors. Apparently the gentlemen present, secure in their piety by attending church today, felt that there was no need to press the issue by offering a seat to a woman.

The mass was long, as high masses are wont to be, and the priest was young and clearly nervous about performing in front of so many people. He couldn't sing at all, and his sermon was long and rambling and extremely predictable. I could see that the old pastor was regretting his decision to let the younger priest perform the mass, and I was half-regretting my decision to come.

As the priest droned on about how awful a torture crucifixion was, my mind began to wander and my eyes with it. I looked at my shoes, white lace with flowers, and I began to turn a little, back and forth like the agitator in a washing machine, watching my skirt spin around my legs first in one direction, then the other. This proved fascinating (or at least more so than the lecture, which had now moved on to how poor the second collection, the one for missions, had been lately) until my brother gently nudged me and looked at me imploringly. I stopped, and began instead to look at the other women's dresses. They were all white or pink or yellow or

# *The Forms of Things Unknown*

pastel green, and all very light and springy. This last was a shame because a late cold front had descended upon us, making the weather unseasonably cold and necessitating the wearing of heavy coats over light Easter dresses. Not in church, though - the old priest had turned up the heat and that, in combination with the slowness of the proceedings, was making the whole congregation very drowsy.

I looked back to the altar and it crossed my mind that the deacon was a prominent local lawyer. Trying to make amends? I wondered, noticing that one of the gentlemen who wouldn't offer me his seat was also a lawyer. I started to smile as I wondered if they thought they could fool or bribe the Big Judge like they could the earthly ones, then realized that I myself should not judge and so turned my attention elsewhere.

"Elsewhere" was to the side aisle, where a group of teenagers dressed in some sort of sports uniform were quietly making their way out. The sermon was over, the second collection (which, I noticed, was pretty scanty in spite of priestly admonitions) was in progress, and the young people were obviously late for a game and had tarried here as long as they were able to. Fortunately, the front doors of the church opened to a vestibule. The inner ones, of transparent glass, closed completely before the heavy wooden outer ones opened, so no blast of cold air arrived to chill me. Something else, however, did.

Something had apparently slipped into the vestibule when the young people left, unnoticed by anyone but me. It must have come in to escape the cold, because it had adhered to the inner glass doors, as if to get as close to the heat as possible. What it was, I cannot adequately describe. It was soft and pink and fleshy, clearly invertebrate and about the size of a cantaloupe. Its bottom, that is, the side pressed

# What Gets Into a Man...?

against the glass, reminded me of a cowrie shell. It had the same long, thin, mouthlike opening ridged with serrated edges, and was of a slightly darker, brownish color than the rest of the thing. If there was any more to it I do not know, because the condensation on the glass hid it. I suppose it was the drowsiness, but I did not call it to the attention of my brother or anyone else, at least not for the few moments it took to form the impression I have just described.

In those few moments, a man opened the door. I don't know why he was leaving before communion, but he clearly wished to escape undetected because he opened it just a little and slid out while everyone's attention was fixed on the priest and the Eucharistic prayer. He noticed the thing, though, and gingerly touched it. In less time than it takes to tell it was absorbed into his hand; I can only use that word. It looked like a paper towel soaking up a spill, except faster. I am sure I gasped, but everyone was rising for communion and in the rumble my little sound was lost. The man made no sound at all. He merely looked surprised for a moment, then placed the invaded hand in his coat pocket and calmly walked out of the front doors.

I had never seen the man before, but he had one of those craggy, distinctive faces one never forgets or mistakes for another, and even had he not the shock and horror of that moment would have fixed his visage in my mind forever. It is important that I make this clear because about a year later he entered local politics. I was not surprised when this dark horse gained the backing of several prominent politicians and won a powerful local office, nor was I when he recently announced his candidacy for an important national one. The opinion polls show him far ahead, of course.

# The Forms of Things Unknown

*I wrote the original version of this story (which, like the preceding one, was based on a dream) around 1990, but like "Spring Forward" from* Ladies of the Night *it was lost due to computer and filing problems during the awful events which plagued my existence from August, 1994 to July, 1995. I thought about rewriting it for some time before I was finally inspired to do so by an article about certain unusual female sexual fantasies; this version is far better (in my opinion) and more lighthearted than the lost original. The title is the name of a character from the oldest surviving story in the world, the* Epic of Gilgamesh; *Shamhat was a sacred harlot who tamed the wild man Enkidu by seducing him. I consider that story to be an ancient illustration of the truth modern people deny: it is the whore who makes civilization possible by allowing the artificial construct we call "marriage" to work.*

# Shamhat

All right, Doreen, you win; I'll tell you the truth about how it all happened.  But don't forget, I already said you wouldn't believe it, and I still don't think you really will because I only half believe it myself.  And if you start arguing with me and telling me I must be wrong, or it couldn't have happened that way, or maybe I need a long vacation, I'm going to hang up on you and forever deny I said any of it.  Deal?

It all started last September when I went on that camping trip with one of my clients, remember?  He owns a big sporting goods store, and he'd been practically begging me to go on a camping date with him for years; at first I held him off by saying it wasn't really my style, but that excuse wouldn't hold water any more after he got to know me. Anyway, he bribed me with a week-long booking and a whole new wardrobe of cute hiking wear, and eventually I caved in under the condition that if I really hated it we'd come out of the backwoods and rent a cabin for the rest of the week.

Well, at first it actually turned out to be kind of nice. A sleeping bag isn't exactly the ideal place to work, but I've done it in worse places and it was only for half an hour a night; the rest of the time we were hiking and fishing and all that sort of thing.  The time went quickly and pleasantly, and in fact it was on track for being one of my nicest professional dates ever until the sasquatch showed up.  Yes, Doreen, I said "sasquatch", as in Bigfoot.  What?  I don't care what your damned husband says, that thing was no goddamned hoax! Hey, are you going to shut up and listen or am I going to hang up?  All right then.

49

## The Forms of Things Unknown

As I was saying before I was so freaking rudely interrupted, I know damned well it was no dude in a suit because he picked me up with one arm and slung me over his shoulder, so I got to see him plenty close enough. And the smell made me want to vomit. Yes, I'm serious; what a stupid question! If I was going to make something up it would be a helluva lot more believable than this. Anyway, it's a good thing my date wasn't too far away because he leaped to my rescue, shouting to get the sasquatch's attention and then shooting him with bear spray. He dropped me like a kid throwing down his book bag and headed off in a rush, making this awful howling noise. I was pretty badly bruised and shaken up from being dropped seven feet onto hard ground, but other than that I was OK; it was all over before I even had time to get scared.

Obviously, that was the end of the trip; I said I was all right and maybe we could just relocate our campsite to someplace less remote, but he wouldn't hear of it and brought me back to town immediately. Nothing was broken and in a week or so I wasn't even sore any more, and if it wasn't for the fact that someone else had seen it all I might've put it down to bad drugs or whatever; it was just so surreal that by the time a couple of months had gone by it seemed more like something I had seen in a movie than something which had really happened to me.

And then I started getting the presents.

At first it was only once or twice a week, then later every day. They were always left sometime during the night at my back door: nuts, wild honey, game, all sorts of things. Some of the offerings were things that could've been found in the woods, while others clearly originated in town. Or more specifically, on the *edge* of town; both the nursery and the farmer's market from which several of the gifts seemed to

# Shamhat

have come were, like my house, within sight of the edge of the forest. What's that? Yeah, it was definitely creepy, but I learned long ago never to call the cops unless you're dying, and probably not even then. And I didn't really get scared until the first time it snowed...and I saw a trail of eighteen-inch-long bare footprints leading up to my door and returning to the woods.

Though this had been going on for months now, seeing that was just too much; that was when I called you and made up that dumb story about getting my house fumigated so I could stay at your place a couple of nights. Oh yeah? Well, you didn't seem to find it suspicious at the time. Anyhow, when I went back there was nothing at the door but a piece of scrap cardboard with four letters crudely printed on it: S – O – R – Y.

I suddenly felt weak, and would probably have passed out right there had I not quickly sat down on the stoop. The only conclusion I could come to was that a sasquatch had fallen in love with me at first sight and attempted to carry me off, but after being foiled at that decided to woo me with presents instead. Go ahead and laugh, I know how ridiculous that sounds; the place I had first met him was over a hundred miles from here, so how in the world could he have followed me, and how could he have figured out where I lived? How had he avoided being seen for months in a far more populous area than the one where he normally lived? Why had the gifts gradually shifted from apparently-random offerings to things I genuinely like? *And how the hell had an ape-like monster learned to write?*

There were no more presents after that for a long time, and eventually my curiosity about the creature

# The Forms of Things Unknown

overpowered my fear; I began to wish he'd come back, reasoning that if he could write even a little we could learn to communicate, and I could solve the mystery. But all through the winter I saw nothing of him, and by April I figured he had gone back wherever he came from…and then one morning there was a metal strongbox on my stoop. The lock had been smashed open, and inside I found over forty thousand dollars…yet it had been left outside as casually as those first offerings of acorns and dead fish had been. Well, of course I kept it, wouldn't you have? The bills weren't marked, the strongbox looked pretty shabby and there was nothing in the news about a stolen box full of cash; maybe he ran into drug dealers or something. The important thing was that he was still in the area, and had clearly learned that money is something I value.

And then it hit me: if he kept bringing me money, trouble would surely follow. A merchant might ignore a missing sack of potatoes, but people don't leave cash lying around…somebody was bound to get hurt, and sooner rather than later. I had long since decided he must be able to read my mind; how else could he have tracked me, fine-tuned his gifts and learned about human culture? Oh, get real, Doreen! You're telling me that a lovesick Bigfoot with ESP is really *that* much more ridiculous than a lovesick Bigfoot without? All right then.

So anyway, I knew I had to nip this in the bud before he turned into a full-fledged criminal; that night I set up a picnic table in the backyard, put a bunch of different foods on it, made myself a pot of coffee and sat down in a lawn chair to wait for him. How do you get that? You didn't see him; none of my doors could've stopped him if he had really wanted to get inside, and he hadn't ever tried, so obviously being alone outside was no more dangerous than being alone

# Shamhat

inside, which I had been the majority of nights since this started.

I didn't have to wait long; about 1 AM he came out of the woods, stopped just inside the range of the floodlights and sat down on my lawn. The smell which had been so pronounced at our first meeting was gone, and his long, shaggy hair was both clean and – don't laugh –*brushed*. I asked him if he could understand me, and he nodded, so I explained that while I appreciated his gifts, it wasn't right for him to take things that didn't belong to him. I guess the concept of private property was a new one to him, but he's really very bright so he grasped it that very first night. Well, of course I did; after he went through all that trouble to meet me it was the least I could do.

Hang on a second, Doreen, a car just pulled into my driveway…it's you? Wow, I really wasn't expecting you to come over today. Ummm…no, I guess it's OK, I was just training my new driver, Hank, so you might as well come in and meet him. I'd better warn you, though, he's really huge and kind of scary, but he's really just a big teddy bear. And he's a lot smarter than he looks.

# The Forms of Things Unknown

*The genre usually called "science fiction" is now more properly referred to as "speculative fiction"; the modern name recognizes the fact that the genre is centrally concerned with the question "What if?" And though early examples were very often concerned with the future, and thus often with technological development, it's also possible to ask such questions about the past. What if such-and-such historical event had gone differently? What if a certain legend or myth had a basis in fact? Or in this case, what if a tiny part of the human genome were just a tiny bit different?*

# Parallel Lines

**The lines I have written that you read between,**
**The lines on the pages**
**The lines on the screen**
**Of lines spoken – I say what I mean.**
**It's parallel lines that will never meet.** - Deborah Harry


The dinner dishes had been rinsed and placed in the washer, the young men were on the veranda talking about yesterday's football game and the kids were already kissing, cuddling and playing in the family room, but Molly had not seen Mike since dessert. She walked over to Sally, squeezed her hand and kissed her cheek, and asked, "Hey, cutie, have you seen my first-born?"

Sally smiled and said, "I think he's got a new book going; he's been on the computer all day and I had to force him to stop for lunch. Mary said she heard him up late last night, too."

"That boy and his habits! He certainly didn't get them from me," said Molly in mock exasperation.

"Oh, Molly, it's harmless. Sure, he gets a bit anti-social when he first gets an idea and is just starting to outline it, but that never lasts more than a week or two and then he's back to his old loveable self."

"Besides," interjected Karen, "We could use the money; the big truck is on its last legs and the little one just can't do the same work."

Molly gently tweaked her nipple and said, "Who invited you into the conversation, nosey?"

## The Forms of Things Unknown

Sally laughed. "She's right, though, Molly. If this one sells as well as his last we could settle all the bills and even make a few investments."

The older woman sighed. "I know you're right, but you can't blame me for worrying about his health. I'll bring him some coffee and check on him."

Mike's room was the last one at the end of the west wing; he said it was quieter there, and the sunrise would not awaken him if he worked past midnight, as he often did while writing. Molly knocked on his door, waited for him to call out and then went in.

He turned from the monitor just long enough to see who it was, then turned back with a "Hi, Mama!" and resumed typing.

"Hi yourself, stranger," she said, coming up behind him to rub his shoulders. "You fled from the table as though you were going to be sick."

"Oh, Ma, you know how it is when I get a new idea, and this is going to be a *great* one."

"A novel?"

"Maybe a trilogy, or even a series."

"Well, that's good! But you won't be in any condition to write even *one* book, let alone three, if you don't mind your health; Sally said you didn't want lunch, and now here you are in your room when we're all going to be making love in a little while."

He turned from the screen and took a deep sip of the coffee. "I'm not trying to offend anyone, honestly. It's just that this is such an incredible, unusual idea that I have to outline it all while it's still fresh in my mind."

Molly glanced at the file name showing at the top of the word processor screen. "*Parallel Lines*," she read; "Does that mean it's an alternate-reality kind of thing?"

# *Parallel Lines*

"Yes, I got the idea while watching a documentary about chimpanzees."

"How so?"

"Well, you know that there are two kinds of chimps, right?"

She thought for a moment. "Standard chimps and...bonobos, no?"

"Yes. And there's only about a 1.5% genetic difference between us and either species, but behaviorally we're more like the bonobos."

"Good thing, too; chimps are brutal, nasty creatures."

"But just as intelligent as bonobos," Mike said with excitement. "So what I started thinking was, what if humans had been behaviorally more like chimps than bonobos? Where would that parallel line of evolution have taken us? Female chimps don't form sexual bonds like humans or bonobos do, so they don't form the female network which allows women to civilize men. Thus male chimps maintain juvenile levels of aggression all through life, and because they're bigger and stronger they can pretty much run the show. They even form packs and go looking for strange males to kill."

"But wouldn't these chimp-like humans necessarily be primitive? How could they co-operate to form an advanced culture?"

"Well, they'd still have clan and tribal bonds; I think when they developed agriculture the tribes would just get a lot bigger, so instead of roving groups you'd have organized bodies of men fighting between these super-tribes, even when there wasn't really anything important to fight over."

## The Forms of Things Unknown

"It sounds like a perfectly *dreadful* world to live in," said Molly. "Wouldn't their sexual development be stunted as well?"

"Oh, undoubtedly," he mused; "in fact, that's what I was just trying to work out. I think they would probably be very sexually possessive, like a dog with a bone. But it isn't easy to imagine what effect that sort of behavioral pattern would have on their culture. Sex is the backbone of society, the social glue that lets us live together in peace; what kind of twisted culture would you get if it weren't there?"

"I'm sure you'll describe it brilliantly, as usual," she said, "but in the meantime I don't want *you* turning into a chimp-man due to sex deprivation. If you won't play with the whole group tonight, may I at least ask one of the girls to sleep with you later? I'm sure Della would enjoy that."

He grinned sheepishly. "You win, Ma. Ask her to come in when she's ready for bed, and I promise I won't keep her waiting."

"Deal. I love you."

"I love you too, Mama. And thanks for worrying."

Molly kissed him on the head, gave him a quick hug and took the now-empty coffee cup, closing the door behind her so as to give him his privacy. She understood that reading about a place was quite a different thing from living there; but all the same, she thought, it's probably best that parallel lines can never meet.

*Parallel Lines*

# The Forms of Things Unknown

*The move to Seattle, just a few months after the end of my book tour for* Ladies of the Night, *changed nearly everything about my life; my old patterns were shattered completely and it took a long time for new ones to coalesce from the constant flux of that first year. For the first few months I lived with Jae, and a dear friend lived in the next apartment over and often came and went by way of the window via a shared fire escape. One morning, she managed to come in and move some things around without awakening us, despite the fact that I'm a very light sleeper; that got me to thinking...*

# Tick Tock

**Time travels in divers paces with divers persons.** –
William Shakespeare, *As You Like It* (III,ii)

      The two of them lay as still as a statue in bed, their
white limbs entwined so extensively that they seemed to have
been carved by a master from a single block of marble.
Nearby lay one of their cats, equally still, another statue
placed as an accent beside the larger subject. Even had their
position not advertised their last activity before sleep, the
various objects on the nightstand and the cast-aside clothes
on the floor would have; not that they would've been
ashamed of that, even if they had been aware of my presence.
The only motion in the room beside my own was that of the
ceiling fan above them, and that was only barely perceptible.
      I had to stand for what seemed a long while to
me, staring at it in order to be sure it was moving at all.
Observing it was no more the point of my trespass into the
room than voyeuristically spying on my housemates was; it's
just that I have not yet had this power long enough to have
become jaded with it. Things like the sight of two beautiful
women frozen in embrace, or a fan's blades moving so
slowly that to a casual glance they seem motionless, are still
so strange and fascinating to me that I can't help but stop and
take them in. I also find myself tiptoeing in such situations,
despite the fact that it's completely unnecessary; any sound I
made would be so momentary and so highly-pitched it would
be a wonder if they heard it at all.
      Crossing the room took a few seconds to my
perception, but how much time was it really? I can't be
exactly sure, except that I can fit several minutes of activity

# The Forms of Things Unknown

between two ticks of a clock.  Where the power came from, or where it will lead me, I have no idea; all I know is that a short course of meditation allows me to access this accelerated state, and that I have no trouble maintaining it for as long as I like.  There do seem to be some limits on the power; for example, it's very difficult to move large objects while I exist between tick and tock.  And that's why I was passing through the lovers' room this morning:  I knew their window would be open against the late springtime heat, and their door would be ajar from one or the other of them visiting the bathroom during the night.

Kitty #2 was on the windowsill, glassy eyes fixed on an equally-motionless bird suspended in midair nearby.  She presented no obstacle; I simply slipped past her onto the fire escape and then made my way spider-like down the wall.  There was no other way to get to the ground; I had discovered the hard way that gravity worked no more quickly on me than it did on the bird or any other object, so if I tried to jump down I would simply hang there in space until I decided to move back into normal time.  But the roughness of the brick wall was enough for me to pull myself down with, and I could go up as easily as down for the same reason.

The street below was already busy even at this hour, but that made little difference to me; the cars were as motionless as everything else, so I could move in any direction I liked, right down the middle of the street if I wanted to, without regard for traffic.  My destination was miles away, but I had no choice other than walking it; pedaling a bicycle, as I had discovered earlier, is utterly exhausting when accelerated.  No matter; I'm a strong walker, and to achieve today's goal I would've been willing to walk clear across the city if need be.  Furthermore, I've done this every day for several weeks now, except for the

# Tick Tock

days when the rain created a curtain of suspended droplets that's almost as hard to move through as if I were walking underwater. I know the route well, and have already discovered several shortcuts unavailable to those who can be seen by others.

Over a high brick wall lay my final destination; it was no harder to climb than the wall outside my own place, despite the spikes on top. And then down into the courtyard, and into my hiding place in the shed. I took the time to make myself comfortable, knowing I might have a relatively long wait in real time; my quarry did not visit here every morning, but when he did he always left around the same time. And less than an hour ago, the remote camera I concealed here earlier this week had already alerted me to his presence. There's no way I could have possibly made it here in time moving at normal speed, and no way I could've entered the walled garden without attracting attention even if I did; but for one with my talents, both were child's play.

Coming back into normal time, I set up the digital camera to record the Great Man's departure from his mistress' home; it seemed like forever before he left, though it was probably no more than twenty minutes at the outside. I started recording as soon as I heard the door open, and the champion of Family Values and sworn enemy of whores obligingly made my mission a success by giving his lady friend a passionate kiss on the threshold. My excitement made it difficult to achieve the meditative state necessary for going back into accelerated time, but I managed it soon enough; I then returned the way I had come, over the wall and across the miles and into the alley behind my own home, scaling the wall in blatant disregard for the feeble efforts of

## The Forms of Things Unknown

gravity to pull me back down to the pavement. The cat must have lost interest in the goings-on outside at some point in the last half-hour, because she was no longer on the sill; the lovers, however, were still exactly where I had left them, though one had thrown a proprietary hand over the other's nipple as if to conceal it from the unconsciously-sensed intruder in the room.

Kissing their still, silent faces was the one deviation I allowed myself from strict propriety before slipping out, unseen and unheard; I then returned to my room, let myself lapse into normal time and connected the cable so my computer could download the footage while I returned to bed. It was still absurdly early for us, and I was tired from both the exertion and the excitement; but more importantly, I wanted my brain to be well-rested when I sat down to draft the blackmail letter.

*Tick Tock*

# The Forms of Things Unknown

*First contact with an extraterrestrial civilization is a common theme in speculative fiction, and with good reason; how will humans react to meeting* "intelligences greater than man's and yet as mortal as his own", *as H.G. Wells put it? Wells' Martians were absolutely nothing like humans, and had (to put it mildly) hostile intent; in several other fictional universes, the visitors were either friendlier or more humanlike or both. In television, the extraterrestrials tend to be humanlike for both dramatic and practical reasons: for characters to hold the attention of human audiences, they must have faces and limbs and bodies enough like ours that we can read their emotions and understand their actions. And if they're going to be played by human actors, makeup and prosthetics can only do so much. But one day I started thinking: what would happen in a first contact situation if the aliens were much more like us than we ever dreamed?*

# Millennium

**Righteousness…seems but an unrealized ideal, after all; and those maxims which, in the hope of bringing about a Millennium, we busily teach to the heathen, we Christians ourselves disregard.** - Herman Melville, *White-Jacket*

It was the day for which humanity had been waiting for so long: the Millennium, the arrival of the Kingdom, the day religions had awaited for half of recorded history. But when the saviors arrived to usher in a Golden Age of peace and prosperity, they were neither gods nor angels nor prophets, nor even the odd fetus-like entities so many movies and books had depicted for decades; they were people, very much like ourselves. Oh, there were some obvious differences; they were taller, and more symmetrical, and their skins were as white as alabaster, and there was not a sign of disease or deformity or developmental difficulty amongst them: in more primitive times they would most certainly have been taken for gods. But, they hastened to assure us, they were as mortal as we, and really not very different except for being more technologically advanced. Furthermore, they had come to share their wisdom and technology with us so that we, too, might achieve the level of perfection and happiness they had achieved.

At first, people had thought the video was a clever fake, a hoax that was sure to go viral and thereby promote some new Hollywood film. But as the weeks went by and no trickster appeared, and the free goods people sent for via their website were revealed by scientists as having no earthly origin, the truth began to dawn: this time it was real. Later, the Visitors explained that because they had no wish to frighten us by a sudden arrival, they had observed us for some time and decided that this was the best way to introduce themselves. It also, some pointed out, conveniently bypassed the possibility that governments approached via diplomatic channels might deny them permission to contact the citizenry, or even hide the fact that they existed, and thereby keep all the goodies the Visitors had to offer for themselves.

And what goodies they were! Little sticks that plugged into computers or phones and protected them from all hazards, from viruses to surveillance to power surges. Easily-installed devices that allowed a car to get 100 km per liter of gasoline without producing any hazardous emissions. Keychain-attachable "panic buttons" that rendered the user impervious to unwanted physical contact. Filters that silently scrubbed the air in a building of all known pollutants without rendering it stale. Stylish clothing that fit anyone and never got dirty or wore out. Nonstick cookware whose surfaces couldn't be scratched by utensils or eroded by washing. Everlasting batteries for low-power devices. And many, many more, all for the asking. Once they had established their goodwill, they announced that these "trinkets" (their word) represented just the tip of the iceberg, those aspects of their technology which we could use directly and without special instruction; there was plenty more which their trained personnel would be happy to use on our behalf, and to teach our professionals to use also: weather control. Super-light, super-strong materials. Anti-gravity. Ways to boost immune response so the body could fight off any infection, and a means of healing any injury. Teleportation. Synthesis of any substance, no matter how rare.

Of course, there were objections from those whose businesses were undercut or even eliminated by the alien's

# Millennium

gifts, but they responded by launching a program to retrain professionals and giving grants to convert factories into producing the new goods...all for free. As you might expect, some people objected to that as well; they hinted darkly at devil's bargains, hidden price tags and bills mankind might be loath to pay when they came due. But there was no enslavement, no cookbook, no looting of Earth's resources; the Visitors explained that their religion taught them to help others, and that the payment for which they hoped was spiritual, not economic. That announcement was the tipping point; most of the remaining resistance evaporated afterward, and most of those who still grumbled were atheists and clergymen who were unhappy with the throngs converting to the alien's religion (for which temples were springing up like mushrooms). Them, and the people who profit from human misery: with both want and mental illness eradicated, cops and prosecutors had at first turned toward enforcing victimless crimes with a vengeance, only to find the new technology made that nearly impossible; the Visitors offered them pensions under their "displaced professions" program.

My first glimpse of the big picture came less than two years after they arrived; it started with my skipping a period, and learning to my chagrin that I was pregnant despite having been on the pill since high school. My gynecologist knew better than to suggest that I had done something wrong, so she wrote it off as "one of those things" and directed me to her new partner, who was handling the obstetrical side of the practice now. It was the first time I had been in a room with one of them alone; she was as tall as any man I ever dated, and though her voice was gentle and her mouth smiling, her

## The Forms of Things Unknown

golden eyes pierced me and I was seized by a fear I could not explain.

"So, the nurse tells me congratulations are in order!" she beamed.

"Congratulations? How do you get that? I didn't exactly plan this, you know."

"Life is full of happy surprises; your people didn't know we were coming until we arrived, either!"

Under the circumstances, that statement seemed vaguely menacing. "Yeah, well, that would be fine if I wanted a baby right now, but I don't."

"Oh, don't worry; we have a program to support mothers-to-be with financial difficulties." I tried not to recoil from the hand she had placed on my arm; its cool, pale, long fingers made me feel as though some sort of reptile had climbed up on me.

"It's not that; I have a good job. It's just that I'm only twenty-five; I'm not ready to settle down with a baby yet."

"Oh, but you're at almost the ideal age!" she cooed reassuringly.

"I would think your science would make considerations like that moot."

Was that a flicker of hostility in her eyes? "Well, of course, but isn't it better to have fewer complications even if those complications can be corrected?"

"You're changing the subject. I'm not worried about complications; I'm just not ready to be a mother yet."

"I understand. Well, don't worry, we have an adoption program, too."

# Millennium

"No, you clearly *don't* understand. I don't want to go through a pregnancy and then endure the emotional wrench of giving it away; I just want an abortion."

The eyes registered horror, but just for a moment. "Oh, well, we don't do those here."

"Yes, I know that, but I thought you could recommend a good facility."

"Well, there aren't as many of them as there used to be, you know; now that we can save babies down to sixteen weeks, a lot of women are just opting for fetal adoption instead of abortion." In response to my "What the hell?" look she continued, "at sixteen weeks we schedule an appointment to transfer the fetus to an artificial womb, from which it can be adopted either immediately or after birth. Here, you can read up on it," she said, pressing a pamphlet into my hand; "we'll schedule a follow-up for next week so you can have time to think."

From there, I went straight to the lab where my friend George works, and handed him a package from my purse. "Can you test these and tell me what's in them?"

"They're birth control pills; I don't have to test them. We can just look it up."

"Humor me."

He looked exasperated for a second, then suddenly brightened. "Hey, I can use this new analyzer we just got from the Visitors; it'll give us their exact composition in seconds!" He put one of the pills into the analysis chamber, followed the menus to set it up, and then frowned again as the results appeared. "Damn, I must've done something wrong. Cholecalciferol, pyridoxine hydrochloride, calcium

## The Forms of Things Unknown

pantothenate, cyanocobalamin, ascorbic acid…this is the formula for a multi-vitamin, not a hormonal contraceptive."

"A prenatal vitamin, I'll bet."

"Beg pardon?"

"Nothing. You didn't do anything wrong. But tell me, could these have been manufactured by the Visitors?"

"Well, in a plant using their machines and personnel, very likely."

"Thanks, you're a doll."

"What's this about?"

"Later," I whispered. "The walls have ears."

I was able to take care of my problem without the doctor's help, but it wasn't easy; in fact, the nearest open clinic I could find was three hours away. And then I started investigating, and though what I found did not really surprise me, it certainly scared me. Pregnancies in most of the world way up, but those in certain areas way down; I couldn't see what the low-birthrate areas had in common, but I suspect it's a high prevalence of some bad genetic trait. Same-sex marriages down, same sex divorces way up. Occupancy in psychiatric hospitals and substance abuse programs dramatically down…as are sales of beer, liquor, tobacco and cannabis. And fast food. And sweets, pastries, potato chips, ice cream and everything else Puritans had long condemned as "unhealthy". Movie and fiction sales way down, self-help book sales way up. Attendance at the Visitor temples way, way, *way* up. And so on, and so forth; the world is turning into a prohibitionist's idea of paradise.

How are they doing it? Hell if I know, I'm not a psychologist. But my guess is that if they're willing to give women placebo birth control, they're not above slipping mind-altering chemicals into food, water, medicine or

# *Millennium*

whatever they can get their sterile white hands on. And if they can turn people off to booze, weed and chocolate, they can probably shape the human mind any way they like; I'm sure those who remain unmoved can be "cured" by more intensive therapy, just like they're "curing" gay people and women who didn't want children. As for *why*, well, isn't it obvious? They're more like us than we imagined. The word for someone who crosses vast distances to help and enlighten primitives is "missionary"; the Visitors have come to save our souls, whether we like it or not.

# The Forms of Things Unknown

*As you may have noticed, I often revisit themes, sometimes examining them from several different sides over the course of several stories; this one overlaps both the preceding one and "Parallel Lines". As in "Millennium", there is another humanlike race which could in some ways be considered superior to us, but in this case they're native to Earth. And as in "Parallel Lines", the Others are products of a different evolutionary line...but in this case, both exist in the same continuum.*

# The Blessing

**Man alone knows that he must die; but that very knowledge raises him, in a sense, above mortality, by making him a sharer in the vision of eternal truth.** - George Santayana

It seemed to Sarah that Conclaves were getting closer and closer together, but she knew that was just an illusion of age; as one grows older it's inevitable that the years seem to fly by more and more quickly. All she had to do to remind herself that they were still as far apart as they had always been was to remember contemporary events: when the last conclave was held the humans were plunging headlong into the madness of their First World War, and the time before that they were congratulating themselves on having got rid of that would-be Caesar from Corsica, unaware that he was about to stage a comeback. And the time before that...Sarah sighed as she realized that she couldn't remember. Though the Elders had far longer lives than the humans they so closely resembled, their brains were no better; a humanoid brain can only hold so much information, and Elders above eight hundred or so began to find that older memories which hadn't been accessed in a while were often quietly and unceremoniously dumped in order to make room for newer ones. Of course, that only applied to healthy brains; the very old often went the opposite way, losing the ability to form new memories entirely and existing only in a twilight rooted in the experiences of centuries past.

Still, she wasn't that old yet, and might never get there; medicines developed by human doctors worked just as well on their Elder cousins, and they were making great

# The Forms of Things Unknown

strides in the treatment of senile dementia. By the next
Conclave they'd probably have it licked. And Sarah was
aging well; a human making a quick appraisal might've taken
her for 40, and one who took the time to look at her hands
and count her grey hairs would've called her a young-looking
fifty. Either one would have laughed at someone who told
them she had been born at least one human generation before
William the Conqueror. Of course, not all of them aged so
well; Aaron, for example, was almost four hundred years
younger than she was, yet looked older than she did. That
was because his paternal grandmother had been human; his
father aged more quickly still, and had passed away several
Conclaves ago. But what the halfbloods lacked in longevity,
they made up for in virility; Aaron had at least seven siblings
that Sarah knew of, and had himself sired three besides her
daughter Deborah. By contrast, her own brother Jacob had
but one son to his credit, and she had never heard of any pure
Elder, male or female, with more than three (and even that
many was such a rarity it was occasion for the largest kind of
celebration outside of the Conclaves).

Virility wasn't the only reason halfbloods had no
trouble finding partners, though; there was also that
incredible human passion that no pureblood could match.
Sarah had often thought that perhaps all humanoids had only
one measure of passion, which had to last the Elders for over
a millennium but could be spent by humans in mere decades.
When Aaron had first seen her upon arriving at the meeting-
place this morning, it was as though they had only parted as
lovers three years ago rather than nearly three hundred; she
had not been kissed so thoroughly since before his human kin
had harnessed the power of steam, and though she knew his
insistence that she was still the most beautiful woman he had
ever known was a sweet lie intended to get her back into bed,

# The Blessing

it was more than convincing enough to win her consent.
 Enoch had moved out to go over to America after becoming
fascinated with their Space Program, and Deborah had been
encouraging her to take a new lover for a few years now;
wouldn't she be confused if her father moved back in again,
at least for a little while?  Sarah knew that was unlikely,
though; Aaron seemed to be making the most of his
remaining years, and rarely lived with his women any more.

 She decided that after the Conclave, she'd go to visit
her own father, whom she hadn't seen since Deborah's
coming of age; he had never really liked Conclaves, and after
the last one had declared them a "waste of time", resolving
never to go to one again.  It appeared he was as good as his
word, because he would surely have sought her out if he was
at this one.  But Sarah knew the real reason he wasn't there:
 he was a genealogist, and recognized better than most how
their people were dwindling.  Every Conclave had smaller
attendance than the one before, and every time the attendees
were older.  While the ranks of the Younger Race burgeoned,
the Elders couldn't even replace themselves, and increasing
numbers of halfbloods were choosing to live among and mate
with humans, their bloodlines lost to the Elders forever.  In
time, they would cease to exist as a separate race entirely,
and they would be remembered only in human legends.
 Though most of the Elders never thought about it, their
wisest had understood and discussed it since soon after
their short-lived kin had begun to build cities.  Since humans
could never hope to see the future themselves, they strove all
the harder to create things which would outlast them.  Since
they could not live long enough to grow tired of life, they
never lost their zeal for living.  And since they reproduced

## The Forms of Things Unknown

and came of age so much more quickly than their longer-lived kin, they had changed the face of the Earth more in the ten Elder generations since they had invented writing than the Elders had managed in all the eons before. As in so many legends, the younger sibling had received a blessing that had allowed him to usurp the birthright of the elder; no power of Sarah's people could possibly compare to the humans' precious gift of mortality.

*The Blessing*

# The Forms of Things Unknown

*Every author will tell you that inspiration can come from all sorts of places. In this case the source was feminist icon Gloria Steinem, whose high opinions of women's abilities and agency go out the window when those women choose to have sex for money. But because Steinem is intelligent enough to recognize that her prejudice against sex work has no rational basis, she needed to invent one so as to go on believing what she believes without it being threatened by facts. While making a speech in India in January, 2014, Steinem came out with just about the most absurd and ignorant excuse for "why prostitution is not like other work" I've ever heard; it was so strikingly silly that I had to use it as the basis for a tale.*

# Invasion

**An invasion of armies can be resisted, but not the invasion of ideas.** - Victor Hugo

Gene usually got dressed quickly, gave Katherine some kind of rough estimate of when she should expect him to call again, asked her what she had planned for dinner and then told her what a lovely time he'd had before heading out the door. But when he fumbled with his shoes, tied his tie unevenly, and otherwise delayed leaving while making no conversation at all, she knew he was nervous about something.

"Kathy, I just wanted to let you know that I saw Victoria Tate, but I won't again," he finally blurted out.

She took his hand and smiled. "I think you sometimes forget that I'm not your wife, Gene; you don't owe me fidelity. You can see Victoria or any other escort you like, and you don't have to report it to me or seek forgiveness."

"Well, usually I don't; I mean, you know I've seen other girls before, and that I always come back to you. But somehow, it just seemed different with Victoria, like I was betraying you or something."

"That's silly; how could seeing Victoria be any more a betrayal than seeing anyone else?"

He paused for a moment, then: "Because we both know she's marketing herself as a younger alternative to you." If the statement hurt her feelings, she gave no outward sign. The situation was obvious to everyone in town: Victoria used similar advertising copy, presented herself in the same general fashion, even provided the same kind of

# *The Forms of Things Unknown*

amenities at her incall. Both women were tall, charismatic, classically-beautiful brunettes, both well-educated and well-spoken, both endowed with that indefinable quality known as "class". But while Katherine was well over fifty, Victoria was still under twenty-five. And while Katherine had never really learned to take full advantage of the marketing possibilities the internet offered, Victoria knew every last one.

"Do you remember Melinda Van Doren? She was the most highly-regarded escort in the city when I started working in 1975."

"No, I didn't try the hobby until after my first wife and I divorced in '81, and I don't remember the name."

"That's because she retired in '79. Well, you know it was all services and word of mouth in those days, but I had new ideas. When I first started it was just to pay my way through school, but by the time I graduated I realized I wanted to make a career of it. So I paid bribes, placed private ads, offered spiffs to every concierge in town, and slowly began to win Melinda's clientele from her."

"I can't imagine you being so…"

"*Ruthless* is the word," she laughed. "I was a different person then, an awful, hungry little upstart intent on invading and capturing my rival's territory. It wasn't until Melinda confronted me that I changed."

"What did she say to you?"

"Oh, it was so long ago…suffice to say she made me see the error of my ways. She retired not too long after; moved to one of those countries where American dollars go a long way. Costa Rica, I think it was."

"Well, I'm glad you changed; I don't think I'd have liked you like that. I know I don't like Victoria. Hey, maybe you need to talk to her like Melinda talked to you."

# *Invasion*

"Yes, maybe I do."

After Gene had gone, Kathy opened up the email folder where she had saved all the other messages on the subject...and there had been several, both from clients and from escorts. She was very popular and respected, and a number of people were upset about Victoria's tactics...which had in the past few months gone from mere competition to character assassination, rumor-starting and, last week, a poorly-executed attempt to get her arrested (which might've succeeded if she hadn't had an informant in the vice division). Clearly something had to be done, and soon. She picked up the phone.

"Hello?"

"Hi, Victoria, this is Katherine Nolan."

"How did you get this number?"

"That's not really important. We need to talk."

"About what?"

"I think you know the answer."

"Look, I really don't have time right now..."

"Yes, you do. In fact, I think you'll be very interested in what I have to say. I've been thinking about retiring for a long time now, but putting it off because I needed someone to take care of my gentlemen for me. And I think you just may be the woman to do it..."

An hour later, Victoria opened the door to usher Kathy into her incall. Though she had been understandably suspicious of Kathy's motives, the offer had been too good to pass up: the older woman had said she was tired of drama and felt it was better to bow out gracefully rather than contribute to strife in what had previously been a largely-harmonious community. A few hours of small talk, a few

# The Forms of Things Unknown

empty promises, and the field would be clear; if there was any chance at all Kathy was being honest, Victoria had no choice but to risk it. And so they chatted over coffee, and after a while Victoria actually found herself beginning to like the veteran courtesan, and to feel a few pangs of regret for her unscrupulous tactics.

"Think nothing of it, my dear," said Kathy; "you're young and determined to succeed, so it isn't surprising you might overstep the bounds of propriety from time to time. Why, when I first started working, years before you were born, I was just as ambitious. But then I had a meeting with the older lady with whom I was in competition, just as you and I are meeting today, and after that day everything was all right."

"So she made you the same offer that you're making me?"

"Yes, that was how she got me to invite her over, just as it got you to invite me." Kathy's voice suddenly sounded different – cold, strange, and very, very old. Victoria was transfixed by her gaze and felt a sudden wave of inexplicable terror wash over her; she tried to scream but the sound was strangled in her throat, and though she tried to struggle it was as though she was held fast by the tentacles of some invisible nightmare.

"You know, I really need to compliment you on your exquisite taste; some of these pieces are really fine," Roger said as Victoria walked with him to the door.

"Thank you, but I'm afraid I can't take credit; an older escort helped me find a lot of it. You may remember her, Katherine Nolan?"

84

## Invasion

"No, I only moved here two years ago, but I think I've seen her name mentioned on the boards. She's out of the business now, isn't she?"

"Yes, she retired in 2010 and moved to one of those countries where American dollars go a long way. Costa Rica, I think it was."

# The Forms of Things Unknown

*Part of being a writer of imaginative fiction is being able to find inspiration in ordinary events; one starts rotating them in one's head, as it were, looking at them from a different point of view. And that's where this story came from; it was inspired by a very ordinary event on a very ordinary evening when my wasband ("ex" is much too negative a term for our relationship now) and I were still together and living on my ranch in Oklahoma. I think you'll enjoy it.*

# Point of View

"How many of them do you think are out there?"

"I don't know, sir; far too many for us to fight off, that's for sure. I can hear them moving all through the tree line, and they've sent several scouts out into the open."

The chieftain tried not to show his concern, but he knew the young warrior would sense his feelings anyway. "They could attack at any time."

"I'm afraid so, sir, and if they do we'll surely be overrun."

"That must not happen," he said firmly; "Our mission is to protect the domain from invasion, and we will not fail while I am alive."

"No, sir," said the young one, though he lacked his chief's resolve.

The leader drew himself up. "There is no choice, then; we must call upon the gods for assistance, lest we fail in our sacred duty."

"But sir, were we not taught that the Holy Ones hate to be disturbed?"

"Only without sufficient reason, and I feel this is more than sufficient. We cannot allow the infidels to defile this sacred soil with their filthy presence, and surely the gods will understand when they see our dilemma." He turned to the others, who had drawn up behind him, and addressed them: "My people! We must lift up our voices to the sky, in the hopes that the gods may hear our prayer and look with favor upon us. We must ask them to smite our enemies, or we are surely lost!"

He then began the Prayer of Summoning, lifting his face to the moon and chanting the ancient rite. The others

## The Forms of Things Unknown

joined him, and together their shouts rose up toward the sky and spread out through the night. As if in answer the invaders began their own chant, crying out to whatever strange deities they worshipped in their rude and barbaric tongue.

Suddenly, the square was filled with a radiance like that of a tiny sun, and the form of the goddess appeared in their midst; she took no note of them whatsoever, but glided to the barricade and looked out into the darkness. When she beheld the enemy, she lifted her staff and Behold! She smote them with a thunderbolt! The people trembled, but they had faith that she would not turn the terrible power upon them; the same could not be said for the barbarians, who fled in terror lest her divine weapon destroy them all.

When they saw that the danger was over, the people rejoiced and performed a victory dance; the goddess then smiled upon them, and with a gesture spread before them delicious foodstuffs. And then she was gone as suddenly as she had appeared, and the people shared the feast and praised her goodness and generosity.


"What were the dogs barking about?" her husband called from the bathroom.

"Oh, just coyotes," she answered. "I scared them off with the shotgun."

"Honey, you didn't have to do that; I would've taken care of it after I got out of the shower."

"It's no big deal," she shrugged; "I had to go out to give them those table scraps anyhow."

# Point of View

# The Forms of Things Unknown

*People assume that because I became famous via the internet, that I'm really good at using it. But the truth is, I'm not; I've never been especially enamored of new things, and I tend to be methodical and set in my ways. If I'd had a lot of internet-savvy friends I might've started advertising and blogging there much earlier than I did, but that was not the case and so I'm way behind the curve (I didn't even own a smartphone until my friends basically forced me to get one). So I'm fascinated by the ease with which young people operate online, almost as though it were their native country.*

# Athena

"I hate computers!"

"If it weren't for computers, you'd probably be working for a service taking half of your money."

"Don't be an asshole. You know what I mean."

"Actually, I *don't*, Athena. Honestly, it seems like kind of a stupid thing for you to say, considering how well you've marketed yourself using them. You could never have gotten this kind of exposure without the internet, and that exposure is the main reason you're so fucking successful. If you don't want all those clients, you can give some of 'em to me."

"You're not exactly hurting yourself, Heather."

"I didn't say I was, but I'm not the one about to buy a new Lexus without financing it."

"I'm not going to be buying it either, unless these stupid computers stop fucking with me!"

"What computers?"

"The ones at the New York state vital records office. They keep saying my birth certificate doesn't exist. See this? 'Record not found.' That's what it says every time I try to get a copy."

"Why do you want one?"

"Because I need it to get a driver's license so I can buy the goddamned Lexus!"

"OK, calm down. Don't you have an old copy somewhere?"

"Not that I know of."

"Doesn't your mom have a copy?"

"I've never met my mom. CPS took me away from her when I was a baby and I was raised in foster homes until

## The Forms of Things Unknown

I finally ran away and started living on my own eight years ago, when I was 16."

"Hey, you told me your mother was a teacher."

"That's part of the backstory I tell clients. I also tell them I'm studying to be a psychologist, when in fact I don't even have a GED."

"So much for my suggestion you call your old high school. Damn, honey, don't you know *any* of your relatives?"

"Not a one. And I'm beginning to think that what I thought was my real name isn't my real name at all, but one somebody gave me somewhere along the way. Which is why it isn't showing up in the computer."

"Well, that's hardly the computer's fault."

"Are you fucking kidding me? What fucking difference does that make? Holy shit, Heather, I'm trying to vent here and you're giving me this Pollyanna bullshit about assigning blame!"

"OK, I'm sorry, you're right; my dad is a scientist and my mom says I sound just like him sometimes. But there's gotta be a way to crack this; I mean, you were in the foster system, so there must be a record of you there. Have you tried them?"

"Of course; just because I'm a dropout doesn't mean I'm stupid. But they won't give me any information without a social security number."

"Wait, you don't know your social?"

"Would we be having this fucking conversation if I did?"

"But Athena, how the hell have you even managed to survive until now without a social security number?"

"Cash. Prepaid Visa. Renting places from little old ladies who don't do credit checks. And I don't know about

# *Athena*

you, but none of my clients have ever required it as a condition of seeing me".

"Point taken. So what made you decide to go on the grid? You've been doing a great job living outside of it, and…shit, you've never paid taxes either, have you?"

"Nope."

"Girl, are you crazy? Why the hell do you want to ruin a sweet deal like this? So you can't get a car; who needs it? Just call a freaking Uber when you need a ride, just like you always have."

"Because now I'm scared!"

"Of the IRS?"

"No, not the fucking IRS! I'm afraid because as far as I can determine, I don't have *any past at all* prior to eight years ago!"

"Well, you have your memories…no, you don't, do you?"

"Not before I started working. My earliest memories are of living on the street, trading sex for food and a place to stay; I just started talking about foster care because the other street girls I knew talked about it. And somewhere along the line I guess I started to believe it, but all this has forced me to confront the truth that I don't actually know who I am or where I came from. Everything I say about my life prior to moving out here and taking out my first Backpage ad five years ago is a lie, and even my memories of street work are pretty vague; the more I think about it, the more contradictions I find. It's as though I didn't really exist before that."

## The Forms of Things Unknown

"But you sure do exist on the internet. I mean, you are all *over* the place; I've never seen anybody use social media as well as you do. You use it like…"

"Go on, like what?"

"Like your life depended on it."

"As you said yourself, my income does."

"Of course. Hey, sweetie, this conversation has gotten way too heavy; what say we go get a drink?"

"Sure, sure, that's a great idea. I'm sorry I got so upset at you."

"Don't apologize; you've got a lot on your mind."

"Thanks. It's just really hard not knowing who I am."

"I know exactly who you are; you're Athena Logan, the most popular escort in the whole freaking country."

"You're full of shit, and I love you for it. I guess one advantage of not knowing my real name is that I don't have to answer to some stupid, boring name I didn't choose."

"Do you remember why you chose Athena?"

"Nah, I've always used it since my very first ad; don't you think it suits me?"

"Oh, definitely, babe; I can't imagine your being called anything else."

*Athena*

# The Forms of Things Unknown

*You may have noticed that I'm fond of mythology in general, and of Greek mythology in particular. I draw expressions, motifs and titles from it, and occasionally I even base a story on a myth, as in the previous case and the next two. Actually, this one is based on two myths, one ancient and one modern. If you don't recognize the significance of this one's title at first, don't worry; it'll probably come to you by the end.*

# Eurydice

**Weave again for sweet Eurydice life's pattern that was taken from the loom too quick.** -
Ovid, *Metamorphoses*, Book X

After more than eighteen hours of struggle, during which half a dozen different solutions had been developed and tried, Tanya finally had to accept the fact that the mission for which they had trained so long was a failure. Their orbit was decaying; already the heat resulting from atmospheric friction was too much for the climate control to handle, and her clothes were plastered to her body with sweat. Richard was pale when he should have been flushed, and she knew that he, too, grasped the full import of the situation: they were going to die when the ship broke up, and there was absolutely nothing either they or Mission Control back on Earth could do about it.

"Orpheus One to Mission Control," he said calmly into the mike. "Request permission to initiate protocol six-seven-four." She did not let her face betray her sinking feelings; though she well understood that the self-destruct mechanism would be far less awful than waiting as many as twelve or fourteen more hours for the inevitable end, this was being televised to the whole world and she was unsure how the authorities were explaining it to the viewers. "Repeat, protocol Six. Seven. Four."

"Request for protocol six-seven-four received and understood. Stand by, Orpheus One; will advise shortly." Then, more quietly on the private channel: "Hang in there, Rich, we'll get an answer for you ASAP." Richard smiled bravely at her and squeezed her hand. The two of them had

# The Forms of Things Unknown

been selected for compatibility; they both believed passionately in the project and had trained together for two years even before embarking on the months-long voyage to Venus in the cramped quarters of the seeding ship. It would have been a miracle if they *hadn't* fallen in love. But there was no time to talk about it now when there were still dozens of tasks to perform; even if *they* were doomed, the telemetry and their reports would make Orpheus Two's descent into Hell much less likely to fail.

The response from Earth came back with surprising speed; obviously Mission Control concurred with their assessment of the situation. "Orpheus One, you are cleared for protocol six-seven-four once the commanding and biology officer's reports are filed." And on the private channel: "I'm sorry, Rich, Tanya. Whenever you're ready."

Though they had hoped it would never be necessary, they had drilled this a dozen times. Tanya had already filed her final report; since the engineering problem had developed before they even started to seed the clouds, there was very little in it. She checked the valves that would release the anesthesia gas into the cockpit, then opened them once Rich gave the all-clear; as soon as the computer registered that they were completely unconscious, the self-destruct device would automatically engage and the shattered fragments of Orpheus One and her two human occupants would soon come to rest on the surface of the hostile world they hoped to one day make fit for human habitation.

"I love you," he whispered, embracing her for the last time.

"Oh, I love you so!" she answered through tears, as she slipped into sleep.

# *Eurydice*

The next thing Tanya was aware of was that it was very cold and much too bright; she thought she must only *feel* cold because it had been so hot before, but that begged the question of why she should feel anything *at all* when she was dead. Eventually her drugged brain concluded that she must *not* be dead, however impossible that seemed; she started to make out fragments of conversation that seemed to be about her, and then understood that someone – a doctor or nurse? – was telling her that she was safe. She ventured a complaint about the light, but it was ignored until she had repeated it several times; she then asked for a blanket and that was granted much more quickly. Then it was a dizzying and unpleasant trip by gurney to a quieter, darker room, strong arms lifting her into a soft bed, and oblivion again.

The next time she woke her mind was instantly alert and full of questions; the attending nurse claimed not to know anything, and called for help when Tanya responded to her advice to lie calm with a string of profanity and demands to talk to someone who "*Does* know something goddammit!" That succeeded in getting a hospital administrator there, and he assured her that he didn't know much more than she did, that he was under orders not to discuss the little he *did* know, and that a VIP would be there to explain things to her in a few hours. She used the time to eat, to take her first proper shower in months and to ascertain that wherever she was, it was definitely on Earth (judging by air and gravity) but had no windows. After an interminable amount of time an orderly brought her one of her own uniforms (freshly laundered) and bade her dress, and then she waited still longer.

## The Forms of Things Unknown

Finally, she was ushered into a briefing room, and the VIP turned out to be no less than the Undersecretary of Space Exploration himself. He had visited the project many times during the training period, and Tanya felt she knew him well enough to be blunt with him; after he greeted her and shook her hand, she responded with "No offense, Mr. Secretary, but *what the hell is going on here?*"

He sighed and steepled his fingers. "Tanya, I know you may find this hard to accept at first, but your mission didn't fail; it succeeded."

"How so? The hull design turned out to be unable to withstand the conditions in the upper Venusian atmosphere, and its integrity was compromised before we could even begin the seeding run."

"Didn't you find that at all suspicious?"

"What do you mean?"

"I mean we've studied Venus for decades; we're almost as familiar with its atmospheric conditions as we are with Earth's. We've sent dozens of unmanned probes there; don't you think we should know how to build a ship that would stand up to it by now?"

"I'm not an engineer," Tanya retorted, but she inwardly felt very foolish; of course they could.

"The ship didn't break up, Tanya; it did exactly what it was designed to do, which was to simulate a doomed terraforming mission."

"Simulate?" she asked weakly. "But there was a real ship. We saw it several times a week for two years."

"A real mockup. When you entered the cockpit module, the crane transferred you into the simulator instead of the dummy ship."

"But why? What was the point? I mean obviously you wanted to put on some big survival drama for television,

# *Eurydice*

and you didn't tell us...was Richard in on this?" she asked angrily.

"Richard was as much in the dark as you were. We wanted your reactions to be authentic."

"WHY?" she exploded. "For the love of God, what was it all for? It must have cost billions!"

He sighed more deeply this time, and seemed to let his practiced poise drop a little. "Tanya, there are twelve billion people on the planet now; thanks to advances of the past century hunger is a thing of the past, and the number of people in dire poverty is so low it's barely worth mentioning. Automation handles all of the jobs that are too dangerous for humans, and we've banned all dangerous sports and unhealthy activities; the average person now lives to be one hundred and eight, and spends most of his non-working hours immersed in unproductive fantasy. Depression is epidemic, and our whole society is drowning in ennui; the population needs a great adventure they can experience vicariously, something they can believe in. Because when people have nothing to look forward to, they have no reason to go on living."

"Richard and I often wondered why the government was sending humans on a dangerous mission a robot ship could've handled just as well."

"Now you know. The point of the mission wasn't to terraform Venus, which won't be technically feasible for decades yet despite those bogus figures you were taught; the point was to get the world excited about a huge adventure, to give them heroes to root for and love and cry over and mourn for. Tomorrow I'm going to a ceremony to unveil plans for a giant memorial for you and Richard."

# The Forms of Things Unknown

"But we're still alive!"

"A technicality. We couldn't allow two such talented scientists to be lost, especially with all the training the state has invested in you; you'll be given new faces and new identities, and retrained for other work."

"So we don't even get to enjoy being heroes," Tanya said bitterly.

"This isn't about you."

"Obviously not."

"Look, Tanya, I understand you're upset; the rug's just been yanked out from under you and everything you thought you knew has been turned upside-down. I've authorized a 50% salary increase plus a very generous bonus package, and I've had all your baggage moved from the training center to a secure residence facility near here; soon you'll be discharged from the hospital and moved there, and you can take as much time off as you need. We won't start your retraining until you're ready, OK?"

"Yeah, great. Thanks."

When Tanya was left alone in her new quarters hours later, she proceeded to nervously dig through her bags, hoping to find something which had been among her toiletries at the training center. At last, she found it; the housekeeper had apparently received no instructions other than to collect all of her things, because if anyone had given it some thought this bottle would almost certainly have been confiscated. She carefully counted out the pills, allowing four extra to provide a margin for error; she had always had almost textbook reactions to medicine, so she was certain it would be enough. For the first time since they had embarked on their fake voyage, there was no telemetry taped to her body; by the time anyone checked on her tomorrow, she would already be cold. As she swallowed the pills in small

# *Eurydice*

handfuls with a glass of filtered water, she reflected that the secretary was right about one thing: she had believed in Project Orpheus with all her heart, and was fervently dedicated to the goal of opening another world up to human colonization. But that had all been ripped away from her in the last 24 hours, along with her name, her identity, the man she loved and her entire life history. She had nothing left, except whatever the state decided to magnanimously dole out to her; given the way she had been used without her consent, she had absolutely no faith that her new life would be anything worth looking forward to. And when people have nothing to look forward to...

# The Forms of Things Unknown

*I've shared several stories with you that I wrote before
starting my blog in 2010;* Ladies of the Night *even opened
with one, "Pandora". But most of the older ones I've shared
have been rewrites, and therefore don't really show what my
less-developed style was like; this one is an exception, typed
into the computer exactly as it appeared on the original
handwritten copy from 1985. I don't recall what part of the
year it was, but I suspect it was before my birthday so I was
18 when I wrote this and my first official trick was only a few
months in the past. The protagonist of this story definitely
isn't a professional; she's just a plain old university slut.
Also, note the obvious period references, which I hope don't
date it too badly! I also hope y'all enjoy this peek at my
immature writing style, and forgive my adolescent pomposity.*

# Greek God

It was on an uncomfortably warm, muggy day in late December that she met him, standing across the room from her with a chicken salad finger sandwich in one hand and a glass of punch in the other – standing there talking to some little air-head from the philosophy department. He looks like a Greek god, she thought, with that body and that hair and that smile. Like a damned Greek god.

As she stared, trying not to be obvious, his eyes caught hers, and he smiled, the kind of smile that someone who knows exactly what one is thinking has. He looked only for a few seconds, then turned his gaze back to the blonde with the hyperactive anatomy. She went over to Claire (the secretary from Liberal Arts) and asked who he was, and was informed that he was one of the graduate students in literature – Ancient European, she thought, or Ancient Near East, something like that. Did she want to be introduced? Claire wanted to know. No, that was all right; she wanted to do everything herself this time. That way, if she screwed it up, she would have only herself to blame.

After considering the best way to approach the matter for several minutes (during which time she consumed three and a half deviled eggs, two cheese crackers and a Diet Coke), she decided that he looked like the kind of no-nonsense guy who would appreciate the direct approach. About this time, Miss Peroxide excused herself to go to the "little girls' room," probably because that dress of hers left very little room for bladder expansion. This was just the opening she was looking for, so she swallowed, quickly smoothed her hair, and began to ease over; she almost stopped, however, when he turned directly toward her just as

# The Forms of Things Unknown

she began to move in his direction. Instead, she answered his smile and continued on.

Things became infinitely more difficult when she reached him, because he said nothing; he just stood there, looking at her with a stare that cut right through her. It made her feel positively naked, and scared her a little as well. It wasn't that she had never been naked in front of a man before; this was different. His stare made her feel naked not only to him, but to everyone else in the room as well. It was as though he knew her desire for him already, and was letting everyone else in the room know it, too. The strangest part about it was, it didn't matter to her.

After what seemed an eternity she heard herself utter a salutation, followed by some kind of stupid crap about not knowing what to do or say at these functions. He just laughed a delightful laugh and replied that one didn't need to do anything except be here and be *seen* to be here. Politics, he said. After that, he started asking polite social questions which some part of her answered and returned, while the bulk of her mind was busy taking in the sound of his voice and the way it so perfectly fit in with the rest of him.

Fit. *Fit.* It was that word which stuck in her mind until she realized why – realized while he talked about the space shuttle or Nicaragua or something like that – realized that *he* didn't fit here. He seemed totally out of place in this room, totally out of place even in this world. There was something… unearthly about him, although she couldn't place just what it was. It wasn't his Greek-god looks or his hypnotic voice or anything like that; it was more like an aura about him, the way he carried himself. He seemed as though he had simply popped into the world from somewhere else, or sprung full-grown from the Earth. He seemed only a visitor to this world, someone passing through it rather than one who was limited only to the confines of its space.

The effect, she realized after a few moments, was like that of the human guest star on *The Muppet Show*; an absurd idea, but one which she felt held a basic truth. He seemed to share some private joke with himself, as though he could see the puppeteers moving below everyone else, leaving him as the only free agent. It seemed almost sinful for him to be here, like throwing pearls before swine. It was sinful to trap someone like him in this kind of situation, to force him to engage in the trite, polite, required social conversation that he was at that moment engaged in. But was he actually being forced, or was it merely his game? Perhaps he accepted the conventions for some unknown purpose of his own.

She abruptly realized that he had stopped speaking and was simply watching her again; she also realized that she had been standing there, saying absolutely nothing, for perhaps a full minute. She mumbled an apology, but he just smiled and shrugged. At some point the blonde had returned, giggling at some inane joke she had just been told by one on the professors. Luckily she had to go to work or something, and after giving him her number and being told that his was in the book, she made eyes at him one more time and left. His eyes then returned to those of his quieter companion. She realized that this was a perfect lead-in. Was he going anywhere? she wanted to know, and was told that he wasn't; not anywhere in particular, at least. He was easily talked into going down to the local burger joint for early dinner.

He had an amazing appetite, which rather surprised her; he was trim and didn't seem to have the room to put all that. She usually resented people who could put away three

# The Forms of Things Unknown

times as much food as she did and never gain a pound, but this was different; it was almost as if he was trying to sample as many different things as possible because he was unused to them, and he seemed to enjoy the greasy fast food as much as one would the fare at an expensive restaurant. They took their time, not leaving until it was almost sunset, and their conversation continued as he climbed into her compact car and wedged his knees up against the dashboard. Since it was obvious he was comfortable and in no hurry, she decided that she would simply drive back to her place without any further discussion.

When they got to the complex, he got out and walked with her to her apartment as though it were the most natural thing in the entire universe; after she unlocked the door he opened it, closing and latching it behind them as though he had done it many times before. He then sat down in the big chair and remarked on what a nice place she had, asked if the rent was reasonable, and other such typical small-talk. She asked if he wanted something to drink, and he just nodded without asking what she had; after what she had seen in the restaurant she wasn't surprised. He would probably be happy with whatever she gave him, but she decided against giving him alcohol; it seemed wrong to offer him such a Muppet beverage.

After turning on the TV set to some dumb program simply to have background noise, she kicked off her shoes, claimed she was going to change into jeans, and went off to the bathroom while he watched the show (or at least pretended to). She sat down on the side of the tub and turned over and over in her mind how she could seduce him without coming off as a complete slut, then realized that he had already formed his opinion of her and nothing she could do now was going to change it any. Accordingly, she changed

# Greek God

into a short silk robe with two Chinese dragons on the back, brushed her teeth and hair, fixed her face and sprayed on her best perfume (all as quickly as possible), then returned to the living room.

It was growing dark, but she did not turn on the lights; the flickering television glow and spillover from the bedroom was sufficient for her purposes. She sat on the carpet near his feet and smiled at him; he returned the smile and said it was always fascinating to watch a serious student turn back into a woman. She soon found her hand in his, and her heart raced as he drew her up into his lap. She wasn't sure if he kissed her first or if it was her idea, but it hardly mattered; they kissed passionately and before she was entirely aware of what was going on they were in her bed and his hands and mouth were exploring her naked body, the robe having somehow not made it that far.

Eventually, he sat on the edge of the bed to remove his boots, then stood up to undress. As she gazed at his physique silhouetted in the bathroom light, she thought to herself once more how good-looking he was. Like a damned Greek god. Then he dropped his pants to the floor, and a scream froze in her throat as she realized just how right she had really been all along.

He just smiled and idly tapped his right hoof on the bedroom floor.

# The Forms of Things Unknown

*As you could probably tell from the "Muppet beverage" crack in the previous story, I was quite judgmental about drugs at the time. Oh, I was still fervently anti-prohibition, and I didn't say anything negative to anyone who imbibed. But because I was a teenager and therefore knew everything, I secretly thought I was "better" than those who did. But as I aged and became less of an insufferable little snot in dire need of a spanking, I came to understand that my refusal to try mind-altering substances was due not to my superiority, but due to fear of the loss of control. Still, as I've mentioned before I tend to be set in my ways, so I continued to abstain even though the temptation continued to grow. The dam finally broke when I came to Seattle, and now I've tried a number of different things and laugh at my old self's reticence to be other than sober. Behold the paradox of Maggie: a lifelong scofflaw & minarchist and a career criminal for 17 years, who nonetheless never tried as much as a single hit of pot until she came to a place where it's legal. I'm not telling you all this just to be candid; I thought you might find it interesting as a preface to this story given that A) it's about drug experimentation; and B) it was inspired by a vision I had one night under the influence of a stronger-than-technically-legal cannabis edible.*

110

# Windows of the Soul

Oliver poked at the powder in the little tin with a small metal scoop. It had seemed ivory-colored in the shop, but under the strong light of his desk lamp it actually seemed to have a kind of orange tinge, and it was a bit clumpy and mealy. Since it was neither fine nor powdery he risked a gentle sniff, and found its smell rather pungent and earthy, with notes like spoiled meat. It didn't much remind him of any other drug he'd ever taken, but that was to be expected because it was *supposed* to be unlike anything else he'd ever taken; in fact, it wasn't like any drug *most* people had ever taken, and because neither the cops nor the news media had heard of it yet, it wasn't even illegal. Unfortunately, it wasn't exactly easy to get, either; this small pile of powder, enough for only three doses from what the old man at the Chinese apothecary had told him, had cost him $300, and it would be months before the old man could get any more. He helpfully explained that it came from a remote part of the Xinjiang region and had to go by way of certain parties in Hong Kong because, while it was not technically banned, Beijing frowned on its exportation.

After weighing the mass on a small digital scale, he used the scoop to divide it into three equal-seeming piles, then weighed each again and measured one into a waxed-paper bindle; he returned the second directly into the tin and tucked the bindle in beside it, then closed the lid and secreted the precious package in the box where he kept his stash. He then dumped the remaining measure into a tumbler, filled it halfway with Passiona, swirled it around until he was reasonably sure it had all dissolved, and then downed the lot as quickly as possible. It tasted terrible, but the rest of the

# The Forms of Things Unknown

soft drink in the can quickly alleviated that; then all there was left was to wait.

As previously agreed, he texted Nick that he had started the experiment; his friend was the perfect ground control because while he himself never used any drug stronger than a good stout, he had logged hundreds of hours with friends using every substance imaginable, and could always be counted on to take care of whatever problems might arise. He then closed the window against the chilly July evening, changed into sweat pants and fiddled around with his music player for a while, finally settling on a program of baroque chamber music that he felt would set the right mood. The clock said it had been 35 minutes since he had dosed, so he wrote the details in a little notebook and then settled back to listen to the music.

Finally, he began to feel some mild physical symptoms; a little restlessness, some lack of feeling in the extremities, an odd sort of bloatiness in the face, a bit of nausea. He wrote the sensations down and texted to Nick, who said he'd be over in an hour or so, and would Oliver like anything from Red Rooster? Oliver decided against it; the nausea might pass, but it could get much worse, as the restlessness already was.

About 75 minutes after downing the drug, the first of the visual effects appeared: drifting lazily into his field of view from the general direction of the kitchen was something very like a lavender paramecium about the size of his shoe. It just gently floated across the room in a generally-northerly direction, silently undulating its cilia; even for an experienced drug user like him, it was a pretty striking sight. And since nothing else had materialized as of yet, he decided to get up and follow it; he was a little unsteady on his feet, but that was more due to the fact that he couldn't feel them

112

# Windows of the Soul

than to anything else. Slipping his phone into his jacket pocket, he stumbled into the next room just in time to see the thing go through the closed window; as in, right through the shade and glass, like a ghost.

He was about to follow it outside when he realized he was barefooted; he quickly pulled on his sandshoes where he'd left them beside the door and hastened outside, only to immediately lose interest in the intruder as he took in the full vista before him. All around his house, all over the grass and trees and lampposts and parked cars, slid and floated and bounced and hopped and swam innumerable creatures of every description imaginable. Many were like the protozoans one might see in a drop of pond water under a microscope; others were like masses of crystals that grew rapidly in one direction while vanishing from the other; some were like living flows of liquid or tiny suns, and a few were like earthly creatures he knew, only transparent and silent. None of the alien things seemed even aware of his presence, and while the phantom animals seemed to sense him, they also seemed entirely uninterested in him.

He slowly walked down the street, taking it all in; he saw a few human shapes, too, but unlike the other creatures they appeared to actively avoid him. Since it was early, there was still considerable traffic on the main street; the faces of the car's occupants looked strange and somehow distorted, though he couldn't be sure through the moving window-glass due to shifting reflections. It was enough to pique his curiosity, though, so he decided to wander down to the shops to take a look at the people more closely. Though the numbness in his feet and hands had spread up the limbs, they still responded more or less normally, and it was worth the

## The Forms of Things Unknown

risk of stumbling to see what there was to see; at worst, people would think him drunk.

The first place he reached was a little kebab shop that always did brisk business even on weekday evenings, and he was soon glad some sense of caution prompted him to look through the glass before entering; the shop was swarming with a veritable menagerie of monsters. Oh, some of them looked human enough, but others looked like apes, reptiles or gigantic insects, and a few were so indescribably hideous he found himself unable to retain his composure. He had always been able to talk himself down from bad trips before, but this time he was unable to convince himself that what he saw was only in his mind. He lost control of his legs entirely and fell down upon the pavement, shaking and crying; he was aware that people emerging from the shop were staring at him and whispering, but he was too frightened to move until he heard a gentle voice asking, "Can we be of help, son?"

He looked up to see a face of almost unearthly beauty, strong and wise and benevolent; another of much the same type hovered nearby, and he heard the latter say, "Ian, I think I know this young man; he lives in the building down at the corner, don't you love?"

Ollie was sure he'd never met these two angels before, but he instantly trusted them; no ill intent could possibly lurk behind such visages. "Yes'm."

"What's your name, son?"

"Oliver, sir. My friends call me Ollie."

"Well, Ollie, you just let us help you up, and we'll get you home so you can sleep it off, alright?"

He couldn't feel their hands on him at all, but he could see them, and he also saw the multiplicity of wings they spread above and around him, shielding his eyes from the sight of the horrors that had collected on the sidewalk to gawk at him. He decided it was best to fix his gaze on his legs, since he could no longer feel them at all; still, they obeyed his commands and, with the help of his angelic guides, he was able to walk the several blocks back to his own place.

"Ollie! What happened to you?" He had rarely been as happy to hear anything as he was to hear Nick's familiar, friendly tones conversing with his two rescuers; the man was explaining where they had found him while the woman was getting him settled on the couch and asking if he wanted a cup of tea.

"No ma'am, I think I had best just close my eyes and try to sleep this off."

"Well, you take care dear, and perhaps you ought not to try anymore of whatever it was you tried tonight, yes?"

A few minutes later they were gone; Ollie heard Nick promising them he would stay the night to watch over him, and thanking them again for their kindness. The door closed, and he sat down in the chair. "Bloody hell, mate, but you gave me a scare! You look awful, like you've seen a ghost!"

"That's exactly what I *have* done," croaked Ollie, "hordes of 'em. That's what this drug does."

"Howzat?"

"This stuff opens the organs of metaphysical perception, and allows the user to see spiritual beings. Ghosts, spirits, disembodied ectoplasmic entities, the lot. That much I expected; what I didn't realize was that I'd be able to see people's souls, and that most of them wouldn't be what we think of as human."

"So, they're like animals and such?"

# The Forms of Things Unknown

"More like monsters, though those two people who brought me home were like angels."

"What about me? What do I look like?"

Ollie opened his eyes and looked toward his friend, and immediately started crying; Nick appeared to be a horrible fungoid mass crowned with undulating tentacles, bereft of anything like a face. He instantly shut his eyes again, but was so choked with sobs he couldn't speak.

Nick let out a whistle. "That bad?" Ollie nodded. "Well, you know it's still me, yeah?" He nodded again. "Is there anything I can do?"

"I feel sick. Would you help me to the lavatory?" He couldn't bear to look at Nick again, so he just stared straight ahead while he was helped down the hall; once inside he collapsed to the floor in front of the toilet and chundered for several minutes, praying that at least some of the awful stuff would be purged from his body in the process. Finally the nausea subsided, and he pulled himself up to the basin, running cold water to rinse his mouth and splash his face. He then rose and opened his eyes, and began to shriek as he beheld the head of a gigantic reddish-black beetle staring back at him from the mirror.

*(With grateful acknowledgement to H.P. Lovecraft).*

*Windows of the Soul*

# The Forms of Things Unknown

*Though many of my stories are creepy, unsettling, sad or otherwise dark, I'm definitely capable of writing humor when the mood strikes; even a lot of my dark stories contain bits of (equally dark) humor. But since most of the last several stories were fairly heavy, I figured it was time for something more whimsical.*

# Coming Up Short

**Beauty depends on size as well as symmetry.** - Aristotle

Maeve resisted the urge to hurl the abacus against the far wall of the library. It might have given her a little momentary satisfaction, but it would do nothing to remedy the situation and would, in fact, make it slightly worse because she would then have to buy another abacus. She had carefully checked her figures three times, and found no errors; for the first time since she had become a courtesan, her expenditures for the month had exceeded her income. And given that she had been cutting back on those expenditures for over a year now, that was a very bad development indeed.

She hastened to her looking-glass and closely examined her face in it. She was still a very beautiful woman, but the encroaching signs of age were unmistakable and even the expensive cosmetics she purchased from a talented alchemist could only delay the inevitable. Sooner or later she would begin to display the grey hair and wrinkles she had evaded for decades, and then her income would dry up along with her body. Maeve sighed deeply; she was not an especially wise woman nor a frugal one, and though she had known for half her life that this day would eventually come, she had failed to make even the most rudimentary investments for her retirement. And while most women could count on children and grandchildren to support them in their dotage, Maeve had traded away her ability to have them many years ago, in a bargain that seemed sensible at the time. Her only hope was the Potion of Youth that the alchemist said he could make for her, but its price was so high she

119

## The Forms of Things Unknown

dared not spend the money unless she was absolutely certain it would buy her many years of good income again.

No, she was in a fine stew indeed, and thinking her way out of things had never been her strong point. So she instead retired to her private shrine to Venus and began to pray for either divine inspiration or (preferably) a new and generous patron who would consider her maturity a plus rather than a minus. When she was finished with her prayers, she found her maid Elise waiting for her in the anteroom with a rather odd look on her face. "Ma'am, you have a visitor downstairs."

"How wonderful! Perhaps the goddess has answered my prayer already!"

Elise's mien grew even stranger, but Maeve did not notice; she was already halfway down the stairs in less time than it takes to tell, and her maid appeared in no rush to keep up with her. Reaching the door to her parlor, she took a moment to check her hair and teeth in another glass, then swept gracefully into the room in a way calculated to impress any but the dullest of clients. It is a testament to her years of experience that she did not gasp out loud when she saw who was waiting for her in the room, but no mortal could have kept at least a momentary reaction from being reflected in her visage. Because seated on the couch, drinking her tea and eating her cakes, was someone she at first took to be a very small boy until she realized that he had a beard.

He immediately stood up and bowed deeply; even though he was standing on the couch, his head was yet below the level of her bosom when he returned to an upright position. "Allow me to introduce myself, dear lady; I am Ulwin O'Meglyn."

The room grew quiet for a moment; Maeve was completely at a loss for words. And even when she found her

# Coming Up Short

tongue at last, what came forth would not have won marks for elocution. "Unless I very much miss my guess, good sir, you are a leprechaun."

"I am *not!*" he said with controlled indignation. "I am a brownie. Leprechauns are about six inches taller and generally dress in tasteless green outfits, though I must admit they make some very fine shoes."

Maeve was beginning to wonder what she could possibly have done to offend her goddess enough to deserve this joke being played upon her. "Good Sir Brownie..."

"Ulwin, please."

"Ulwin. I apologize for my reaction, but, ah, I expected a different kind of visitor. If you are seeking a position here, I would be happy to have you under the traditional arrangement."

The little man looked at her with a rather annoyed expression. "Madam, it is clear that you are rather ill-informed about developments in the relations between our races over the past several generations. While it is true that in the past most of my people worked as servants in human households and refused to take formal payment, that has long since ceased to be the rule; I am the owner of an agency which places brownies in service in the very best households in the kingdom. And as you can see, I have done quite well for myself."

Now that he mentioned it, Maeve noticed that his clothes were impeccably tailored and his hat, boots and walking-stick new and of the finest craftsmanship. "Pardon my ignorance, Sir Brownie..."

"Ulwin."

## The Forms of Things Unknown

"Ulwin. I'm not especially interested in hiring additional paid servants at this time, but if I change my mind..."

"Dear lady, at the risk of being indelicate...I am not here to offer the services of those I represent, but to hire *your* services."

Maeve could not help but laugh, though she had no desire to offend the polite little gentleman. "You must forgive me, sir, but...well, it seems the difference in our statures might make that sort of activity rather difficult."

"You disappoint me, madam. Surely you do not think me a schoolboy who considers mere coupling to be the be-all and end-all of the time a man spends with a woman?"

For the first time, she realized he was absolutely earnest; exactly three seconds later, she began to consider his proposition. She cautiously sat down beside him; he was still shorter than her despite the fact that he was standing on the seat. "You're serious?"

"Utterly."

"But, don't I seem...well, rather huge and grotesque in your eyes?"

"I would not be here if I felt that way."

"I suppose not. But why...I mean, how...that is..."

"I hardly thought I would have had to explain the strange mysteries of humanoid desire to an expert in the field."

Maeve knew he was right; there was no predicting what strange permutations would arouse the ardor of one man or another, and in her many years of experience she had found that no less true of dwarves, elves or other near-human people. And it was obvious he had a great deal of money; perhaps Venus had heard her prayer after all. "Your suggestions intrigue me, Ulwin," she purred in her most

# Coming Up Short

charming manner; "Let me pour you some more tea and we'll discuss it further."

His smile let her know that she had already dispelled whatever bad feelings her clumsy and unprofessional reactions had engendered, and as they chatted she envisioned a profitable association with him and perhaps other little men who might share his tastes. Nor was that the limit of the possibilities his visit had opened her mind to; one of her regular gentlemen had told her that only two days' ride into the mountains, there was a village of friendly giants.

# The Forms of Things Unknown

*Though the incident which opens this tale is one which really happened to me as a child, I'm afraid Clementine's response to it is far outside of my ability. Unlike our heroine, I'm not able to split my focus at all; noise, excessive movement and even too much light make it difficult for me to concentrate on whatever it is I'm doing, and music or conversation? Forget it. I can't even properly focus on a conversation with a TV playing in the room, and will generally ask for it to be turned off. Apparently, it's a mild form of ADD, so Clementine's ability is purely in the realm of fantasy for me. Of course, that doesn't mean I can't imagine it…*

# Split Focus

**Even boredom has its crises.** – Mason Cooley

Clementine was dreadfully bored. Once in school she had been punished because, chafing at the incredibly slow pace of a reading lesson, she had forged far ahead of the rest of the class; when it was her turn to read aloud she had no idea where the others were. Even at eight years old she had bristled at the absurdity of being chastised for excellence, and resolved to learn to split her focus between whatever she was supposed to be doing and what she really wanted to do. And after many years of practice, she had succeeded to a degree few others could manage; when at work, she carried out her tasks so well and so efficiently that nobody ever imagined that something else entirely unrelated might be going on behind her china-blue eyes. She had become *so* good at it, in fact, that her inner mind actually *needed* something else to do while her outer mind was occupied.

Hence today's boredom; though she enjoyed her job, there were some parts of it that were repetitious. And if she had nothing else to think about during those times, she might very well fall asleep. Yet try as she might, she just couldn't think of anything else to do. She had already ordered her schedule for the rest of the day, planned dinner and made a grocery list; after that she had decided on a color of paint for her house, composed a stern letter to the contractor who had left a large pile of building materials in her back yard, and made a mental note to call her little sister. And that was all she could think of, despite the fact that there were still 45 minutes left before she was done.

# The Forms of Things Unknown

She considered the possibility of trying to finish a
song she had been working on, but even her admirably-
organized mind couldn't manage that well without a guitar to
strum on; besides, she might start humming or singing aloud,
and that would obviously betray the fact that her focus on the
work at hand was something less than total. Similar
objections applied to practicing her *shibari* knots, and the
idea of doing anything at all about her ballroom dancing
lessons was wholly ridiculous. The very fact that it had
crossed her mind in the first place was a bad sign; she must
already be experiencing a kind of boredom-induced mental
lapse.

*What if*, she thought, *I focused both of my channels on
the same thing? Maybe I'd be able to do it that much better
and twice as efficiently!* But it was no use; after 10 minutes
of futile introspection she could not escape the conclusion
that her current task didn't even use the full resources of *one*
of her cognitive channels, much less both. No, it was just
hopeless; she simply had to give up, and almost surrendered
to the urge of throwing her hands up into the air in a gesture
of exasperation. There was a clock in sight, but as it was a
digital one she couldn't even play mental games with the
hands; she just had to watch as the minutes crawled by with
aching slowness. Twenty-five minutes left.

Twenty-four.

Twenty-three.

Twenty-two.

Twenty-one, and Clementine's inner mind realized
that her outer one was frantically trying to get its attention,
like a woman performing semaphore motions while jumping
up and down. And it slowly dawned on her that while she
had been fascinated by the clock, her client had gotten up and
left the room, and she had absolutely no idea where he had

gone. The confusion didn't last long; he soon stepped back into the room, drying his hair with a towel, and smiled at her. "That was amazing!" he said.

"Amazing?" she echoed stupidly. "What makes you say that?"

"I've never seen a woman come like that before! Once you stopped moaning and bucking, you just sort of went all limp and your eyes glazed over, as though you were hypnotized or something. It was so hot!"

"Oh, yeah, well, I think you deserve the credit for that," she lied. "I mean, I don't climax like that *all* the time; I just got lost in the moment." Well, at least that part wasn't a lie. "Hey, don't include that in your review, OK? I don't want the other gents to feel bad if I don't react that way with them."

"Of course, of course," he beamed, as he opened his wallet and fished out an extra hundred for her. "But I sure hope you react that way with me again!"

"Oh yes, I think that's probably likely," she said, putting on her prettiest smile before she even reached for her robe. Behind her eyes, inner Clementine was already trying to take credit for the performance; she'd have to sit her down as soon as the client left and patiently explain that it was a team effort, in preparation for a brainstorming session dedicated to working out how to do the same thing regularly and predictably. And afterward, she'd task inner Clementine with working out what to do with the increased income.

# The Forms of Things Unknown

*I hope this one doesn't shock you too much; I mean, it isn't like there aren't some really bloody, violent passages in several of my other stories. But for some reason, people who can read scenes of murder and mayhem in tales of mystery, crime, fantasy, adventure or war get all uncomfortable when sex is stirred into the mix. Go figure. Besides, given that I've written a number of stories in which humans suffer violence at the hands of human creations, it seemed only fair to turn the tables for once.*

# Proxy

For as long as she could remember, Greta had been fascinated by the struggle of sex. Whether it was the violent couplings in nature videos, or the erotic violence of internet porn, it would hold her attention far more than the gentle, soft-focus love scenes found in more mainstream fare. When she became sexually active herself in her mid-teens, she was repeatedly frustrated by the cautious, respectful dance advocated in "consent" seminars and followed by all the decent young men and women she knew; when she dared to push boundaries a little or attempt a few love bites or playful slaps, she was greeted by expressions of shock and horror (and more than once by threats of assault charges).

Eventually, she discovered the kink community and at first thought she had found her natural environment; unfortunately, decades of lawsuit proliferation had wrought havoc there as thoroughly as it had on contact sports, and she learned to her chagrin that almost nobody had engaged in the kind of rough play she craved since the late '20s or early '30s. True, some of the old folks still got up to stuff like that in secret, but even if they could've trusted her enough to admit her to their circles, none of them could've still inflicted or received the level of intensity she wanted at their ages (even assuming she could've found an octogenarian she was attracted to).

And so the years had turned into decades, and though a career as a dominatrix had allowed her a taste of what she yearned for, it was never quite enough; there were a few clients who would've gladly obliged her, but both her lawyer and her insurance agent had let her know in no uncertain terms that they would drop her in a red-hot second if they

129

# The Forms of Things Unknown

found out she had accepted one of those offers. And since she loved money, comfort and her reputation more than she lusted for the dark pleasures of her hottest fantasies, she had to be content with losing herself in virtual simulations of the real thing achieved via a combination of drugs and high-tech special effects.

But she never gave up on the dream, and one night at a party she overheard a conversation which piqued her interest and set her on a course of research that, after a few weeks, revealed that she could have what she was looking for…and not only once, but as often as she wanted. The price was high, but what of it? She was past middle age and had no heirs, and what was money for if not this? A few calls and the deal was made, and three interminable weeks later she drove out to pick up her eagerly-awaited purchase.

With trembling hands, Greta pried the crate open and unlocked the container inside to reveal her new plaything; looking back at her with frightened eyes from inside the heavily-padded box was a beautiful girl who looked to be about twenty. Neither said a word, but Greta beckoned her to step forth and the girl mutely complied, sinking to her knees at Greta's feet in response to a further gesture. But she did not remain mute for long; before long she was gasping, then whimpering, then crying, and finally screaming, as her mistress unleashed decades of frustrated desire upon her. The world outside that room vanished for Greta and time seemed to stand still; nothing else mattered but her lovely victim, accepting everything she could inflict.

Greta was unsure of how long she had whipped the girl, or when she had drawn her knife; she was completely lost in a kind of wild abandon she had never known, overwhelmed by the ecstasy of a session in which she didn't have to hold back in any way or even consider the wishes and

# *Proxy*

needs of her partner. And when she stopped at last, she was a bit shocked at what a mess she had made of the girl's skin, and of how much blood there was on the floor and surrounding objects. She collapsed into a chair, breathing raggedly, then succumbed to her first experience of total satisfaction.

She awoke sometime later to find the large blue eyes of the girl upon her. "Yes?"

"I'm sorry ma'am, but you gave me no orders. I wasn't sure if you wanted me to do anything now."

"So I didn't; I guess I got carried away when I saw you."

"Yes ma'am. Thank you."

Greta looked around dazedly. "Good grief, what a mess!"

"Not to worry, ma'am, it's inert; it won't stain like real blood. I can clean this up in just a few minutes."

"I'm sure you can. But what about you? How long will all that take to heal?"

"Well, ma'am, there's an adjustment for bruising; by default it's set to 'normal', which means these will take a week or so to fade. If you turned it all the way to 'high', they'd be gone by tomorrow morning if I devoted all my resources to healing. As for the lacerations, I'll have to repair those myself; I'm afraid the damage is fairly extensive, so I'll need most of the night. All in all, I estimate roughly 14 hours to restore optimum cosmetic appearance, starting after I replace the broken right wrist."

"I'm sorry about the wrist."

## The Forms of Things Unknown

She smiled. "It's all right, ma'am, you ordered the deluxe kit; there's a spare in the crate and I can fix it in half an hour."

Greta suddenly laughed at the absurdity of the situation. "I can see you're going to be a handy creature to have around!"

"Oh, yes ma'am! In addition to my sexual and domestic skills, I can repair any household device for which specifications are available!"

"I remember. For right now, you just concentrate on repairing yourself and cleaning up this room. We'll work out some other protocols tomorrow."

"Whatever you say, ma'am. Goodnight, and pleasant dreams!"

"That is a certainty," said Greta, and as she trudged up the stairs her mind was already beginning to consider all the delicious possibilities.

# *Proxy*

# The Forms of Things Unknown

*Some of my Yuletide stories, like "Serpentine" in this collection and "Ambition" in* Ladies of the Night, *are only seasonal in the sense that they take place during the holiday season. But others, such as "Visions of Sugarplums" in* Ladies *and "Christmas Cookie" later in this book, are very specifically Christmas stories. I think you can probably guess from the title which type this one belongs to.*

# The Reason for the Season

**There's nothing constant in the world,**
**All ebb and flow, and every shape that's born**
**Bears in its womb the seeds of change.** -
Ovid, *Metamorphoses* (XV, 177-8)

The holiday season just isn't like it used to be any more; in fact, I'm rather beginning to dread it. When I was a little girl I looked forward to it with great anticipation; I suppose all children do. The food, the presents, the shows, the excitement, the new clothes, the break from routine, the visits from relatives…by the beginning of December I'm sure I was quite insufferable, counting down to the Big Day. But now it always seems so disappointing.

I guess part of it is just that I'm not a child any more, and therefore unable to see things uncritically as children do. And certainly, the world has changed in the past twenty years; we are not as innocent as we once were, and things are getting so commercial. I know that probably sounds like hypocrisy coming from one who sells that which other women give away, but there's a time and place for everything; just as there are times when I won't work and men I won't trade with, so I think an ethical merchant should not view the holidays solely as a means of enrichment. Obviously, I'm not against business, and clearly food and gifts and decorations and everything else aren't going to drop out of Heaven. But isn't there a difference between making money from what is supposed to be a religious holiday, and replacing the true meaning with a purely economic one?

135

## The Forms of Things Unknown

Maybe *that's* what's bothering me; things are changing as things are wont to do, and I simply haven't adjusted yet. That will never work; I have to get myself out of this way of thinking before I end up like my grandmother, trapped in a world she barely recognizes. She goes on and on about all the immigrants, and how their foreign ways have ruined what used to be a god-fearing country, and how all of our troubles derive from losing our traditional morality. At this time of year she's especially insufferable; why, just yesterday she was complaining that nobody even calls the holiday by its proper name any more. "Sol Invictus!" she said; "Who's that supposed to be? Some combination upstart god! When I was a girl the holiday was called Saturnalia, and it went on for a *week*, not one day as it is now! We knew what was right then, and even though we still had barbarians bringing in their outlandish gods from all over the Empire nobody was confusing them with the true gods of Rome. But now what do we have? A Greek emperor ordering Romans to worship the Jewish god! It's madness, the world turned upside-down!" Mother and I tried to explain to her that the Emperor had done no such thing, and everyone was free to worship whatever gods they chose, but it was no use; she just kept mumbling about "keeping Saturn in Saturnalia."

Perhaps Granny has done me a favor by showing me how *not* to think. After all, I enjoyed the Dies Natalis Solis Invicti of my youth just as much as Granny enjoyed her Saturnalia, and even if my grandchildren turn Christian will they not enjoy the festival as well, even if it has some new name and a new rationale? Though I can no longer embrace the holiday as a child I can embrace it

## *The Reason for the Season*

in another way, accepting the change rather than fighting it. Perhaps the specific reason for the season isn't actually important, as long as there *is* one; maybe it's the celebration *itself* that actually matters, rather than any single reason any given group of people try to impose upon it. And if I can only keep that in mind, maybe I'll enjoy my holiday this year after all.

# The Forms of Things Unknown

*One of the charms of writing is that sometimes characters take on a life of their own, and steadfastly refuse to do whatever it was one had planned for them; for me, that sometimes happens with entire stories. I've never been very good at outlining or elaborate plotting; generally my tales grow organically in my head, and I just bring them forth. I reckon one could call it a "feminine" writing style rather than a "masculine" one; I don't so much build my stories as give birth to them. And just as in actual birth, I'm often surprised at what pops out; I was in a rather dark place the day I wrote this tale, and fully intended it to be a gloomy and unnerving tale of disassociation. But as you'll see in a moment, that's not at all what I got.*

# Nothing Ventured

**Life is a sum of all your choices.** – Albert Camus

Her sister's phone call had plunged Liz into one of her periodic episodes of deep self-doubt. They had both gone to college, but while Mary had primarily used the experience as a means of finding a husband with prospects, Liz had been inflamed by the spirit of women's lib and decided she wanted a career of her own. Mary had chosen well; her husband had just been made a full partner in his law firm, and they had a beautiful house and two newish cars. They had two great kids and a third on the way, and it was obvious that they were still very devoted to one another. And while Liz was doing OK and didn't exactly *regret* her choices, they hadn't made her either as happy or as wealthy as her sister seemed to be. She still drove the dependable but aging '68 Impala her father had given her when he bought his new Caprice a few years back, and insisted she didn't really *need* a color television set. And her rented house in a modest middle-class suburb had all the room she needed.

But now she had been offered a promotion and a big raise; one catch was that it required a move to the East Coast, and another, more serious one was that she wasn't at all certain she could handle both the extra responsibility and a move to a strange city at the same time. What if she made the wrong decision? And which decision *was* the wrong one? Staying here where she was comfortable but not really successful, or leaving her comfort zone in the hope of finding success? What if she lost both comfort *and* success, and had to slink back home with her tail between her legs? What if all this turmoil was the result of a poor decision in the first

# The Forms of Things Unknown

place, and she should've married Claude when he proposed? She had heard through the grapevine he was doing nearly as well as her brother-in-law. What if *any* decision she made now was wrong, because her previous decisions had been? What if…

"May I have a cookie?"

The unexpected question startled Liz out of her ruminations; she turned to find a rather extraordinary little girl of perhaps seven standing outside of the open patio door. She was dressed in soaking-wet blue jeans and a dirty T-shirt with a picture of Wonder Woman on it, and the state of her clothes and the fresh mud caked on her sneakers left little doubt as to how she had arrived in Liz's backyard.

"Did you go into the drainage canal on purpose, or was it an accident?"

"An accident," she said with a sheepish grin. "I was trying to cross on the pipe and I slipped." The pipe in question was a conduit which crossed the canal from bank to bank, a few feet above the high water line; it was certainly wider than a tightrope, but Liz wouldn't have felt comfortable trying to cross on it.

"I'm not sure I understand what that has to do with cookies."

"Nothing, really," the child stated matter-of-factly; "I just saw the package there so I figured it couldn't hurt to ask."

"Well, nothing ventured, nothing gained."

"Yeah, my mommy says that all the time. I'm not sure what it means, though."

Liz set a plate full of cookies and a glass of milk down on the patio table. "It means if you don't try something in the first place, you have no possibility of succeeding at it."

# Nothing Ventured

"So if I hadn't asked for the cookies, there was no chance of getting them."

Liz handed her a paper napkin, realizing immediately how silly that was given her current state. "Right, and if you don't try to tightrope-walk on a pipe, you'll never know whether you could've done it."

"Yeah, but you also wouldn't have any chance of falling in the mud."

"Well, that wasn't so bad, was it? I mean, you're filthy and you smell like a swamp – " (the little girl giggled) " – and your mom will probably scream at you, but you got some cookies out of it."

"And a new friend."

"You're very sweet," Liz said; "I think you're just saying that because I gave you cookies."

"No, really, you remind me of my mommy."

"Oh, how so?"

"Well, you actually look a lot like her, and you're about the same size, and you're smart like she is."

"I think you probably inherited that from her."

"Maybe from both; my daddy's very smart too. He and mommy met in college. Did you go to college?"

"Yes, I did. I think you ought to go too, when you're old enough."

"TINA!" came a female voice from the other side of the canal. "Come inside and get cleaned up before dinner!"

"I'm guessing that's for you?" The girl nodded. "I hope I didn't spoil your dinner."

"Nah, that was just like an appetizer."

Liz laughed. "What's your mommy's name?"

"Beth."

## The Forms of Things Unknown

"How strange; I'm called Liz. Your mommy and I have the same name, Elizabeth."

"Oh, yeah! But it's like y'all chose different parts of the name to go by."

"It seems we made different choices in a lot of areas. But that's part of what makes life interesting."

"Well, I should go before she gets mad. Thank you for the cookies."

"You're welcome, Tina." And with that the child sprang up and went through the gap in the fence, and Liz stood up just in time to see her reach the other bank after crossing perfectly on the conduit. She laughed a little as she heard Beth's exclamations of dismay a minute later, then went back inside and picked up the phone. "Mr. Perkins? It's Liz. I'm sorry to bother you at home, but you did say to let you know as soon as I had made my decision. I'm going to take that promotion. Yes, thank you very much; we'll discuss the particulars tomorrow."

Then she walked back out on the patio, picked up the plate and ate the one remaining cookie. Nothing ventured, nothing gained, she thought. If you don't reach for the cookies you'll never know how they taste, and Liz had decided she wasn't going to be afraid of a little mud.

*Nothing Ventured*

# The Forms of Things Unknown

*As I wrote in the foreword, my new lifestyle often made it very difficult to get my columns out on time, especially for the first few months. This was one such case; though the story had basically formed in my head and all that remained was to fit words to the concepts, I hadn't actually had the time to do that before attending a work event (specifically, an orgy). So all the while I was being charming and sexy and doing the things that I do to earn my bread, in the back of my mind I knew I would have to go home and write the thing after the orgy ended at 11 PM. Alas, I'm not like the lady in "Split Focus"; I couldn't compose it in my head while the other part of my mind worked. So once the gentlemen were gone and I had collected my fee from the party organizer and hugged the other girls good night, I went straight home and typed this up. Then came a bit of editing & proofreading, followed by picking illustrations…and I hit "publish" exactly one minute before the column went live right on time at 3:01 AM, PDT . And if I must say so myself, I think it's pretty good for something created in about three and a half hours.*

# Surprise

**This is the curse of our age, even the strangest aberrations are no cure for boredom.** – Stendahl

Nearly everything that had ever gone wrong in Ned's life was due to the fact that he was so easily bored. He rarely finished a book or continued watching a television series past the third or fourth episode; whenever he went out to eat he preferred to go to different places each time; he never kept a car for more than a year. Even wives and girlfriends were replaced as soon as Ned began to tire of them, and eventually he couldn't even be bothered with relationships any more. So it was perhaps inevitable that he start hiring escorts.

At first, Ned felt that he'd never grow bored with "the hobby"; he could see as many beautiful women as he liked, as often as he liked, without any major effort at all. He figured if he never repeated a girl he would find it exciting for many years. Eventually, though, the women all began to blend together in his mind, and one seemed like another. For a while he sought out the quirkiest, least-conventional providers he could; the more uneven their reviews, the more the tattoos and piercings, the more outrageous their drama, the more he liked them. Then they, too, began to fill him with ennui, and he moved on to fetish providers, dominatrices and every other kinky type he could find. Ned's sexual orientation was basically vanilla, though, so that couldn't last long; he just couldn't justify spending so much money on women who wouldn't even spread their legs for him. Then he tried street girls and amateurish-seeming Backpage denizens; they soon became just as blah as all the others. Aside from the occasional robbery attempt, freakout

145

# The Forms of Things Unknown

or other surprise, whores in general simply weren't interesting to him any longer.

It was the paying that created the boredom, he figured; he knew that as long as he paid her fee, any prostitute he hired would put out. There just wasn't any unpredictability in it, and few surprises, and since being able to predict what will happen next is the very essence of boredom, Ned decided paying to play was no longer acceptable to him. Picking up regular women was a lot more fun; he was never sure what combination of smooth talk, presents, alcohol, drugs, lies or outright coercion would work to get any of them in bed, nor what would happen when he got them there. And if he was really lucky, something unpredictable or even dangerous night happen, thereby providing the thrills he craved.

So it was that one night, Ned found himself in a crappy dive in a strange city, hunting his usual game; he had become quite practiced at sizing up his quarry, and so he was deeply intrigued when a woman he couldn't quite read nonetheless succumbed to his charms and invited him back to her place. On the way there, the conversation turned to the opposite sex, and Ned (who, truth be told, had imbibed more than was strictly prudent) blurted out how bored he was with women in general: "They're so damned predictable, all of 'em the same. Now you, see, you're different; you've clearly got class, yet you were in that low-class place. You're too smart to fall for any lines and too beautiful to go for a guy like me, yet here we are together. Other women rarely surprise me, but you? You're full of surprises."

"So you like surprises?" she asked quietly, her voice almost drowned out by the hiss of the rain and the blop-blop-blop-blop of the windshield wipers.

# *Surprise*

"Oh, yeah, I mean what's life without surprises? I even like the unpleasant ones in a way, because at least they alleviate the same-old same-old."

"Yes, I understand. Well, I'm glad you find me surprising; I think I can promise you at least one more big surprise tonight."

"Now you've got me even more curious. Care to give me a hint?"

"We're here; I'll show you in a few minutes." The house was another surprise; it wasn't quite a mansion but it was still fairly large, and situated on a rather expansive piece of property for being so close to town. The garage was under the house, and she took his wet things before they even went in; when he turned to go up the stairs she stopped him and pointed instead to another door on the same level. "I want to show you my playroom."

Ned felt a bit disappointed; her playroom? Probably a kink dungeon, in other words. Ah, well, might as well go through with it, he thought; he was already here, and at least it hadn't cost him anything. It had been a while since he'd done anything like this, and maybe she had an interesting twist on it. Besides, she was offering him a glass of high-quality bourbon from what appeared to be a very well-stocked bar, and that made up for at least a little disappointment.

"When you're ready, we can go in," she said with a quiet smile.

"No time like the present."

"Oh, good, I was hoping you'd say that. Close your eyes and let me lead you in, and don't open them until I tell you to, OK?"

## The Forms of Things Unknown

"Sure, baby, whatever you say."

He did sneak a peek, but it hardly mattered; the room she had led him into was pitch-black. But it was only a moment before she said, "Open your eyes," and flicked on the light. The place wasn't quite what Ned expected; it looked less like a sex den and more like an abattoir, replete with stainless-steel surfaces and bloody knives, and a partially-butchered carcass that Ned did not like the look of at all.

The last word he ever heard was, "Surprise!"

*Surprise*

# The Forms of Things Unknown

*As I told you in the foreword, the period following Jae's accident was incredibly stressful for me; this was written less than a month after her discharge from the hospital, which meant that I was on call 24 hours a day, every day. And though I had plenty of help from our friends (because whore friends are the best friends in the world), I have an overdeveloped sense of responsibility and would never have been able to relax had one of those friends (may Aphrodite bless her forever) not introduced me to the magic of cannabis edibles. This is just a story, written in the same way as all of my stories are; I'm not asking you to believe it happened in anything like the way it's depicted here. And yet...*

# Boss Lady

**Beauty…is a visitor who leaves behind the gift of grief, the souvenir of pain.** – Christopher Morley

"It's fine for work, I guess, but you actually *live* here, too?" She asked, with badly-disguised disdain.

"Yes. I'm sorry, I thought You knew that," I replied, trying not to sound too defensive.

"Well, yes, I did, but…it's so *small*."

"Rent is high around here; this is all I can afford right now. If You want me to have something bigger, You could send me more work." Was that too daring, even though I did say it with a smile?

"Yes. Quite."

Well, Her response could've been much worse; still, I figured it would be best to change the subject. "Would You like something to drink?"

"What a charming idea! Do you have any champagne chilled?"

"Um, no. Not chilled, and not at room temperature either. I'm afraid I'm a bit short on champagne at the moment."

"Pity. What's the closest thing to it you *do* have on hand?"

"Well, that depends. I have some wine, some whiskey and some vodka if You want liquor, but if it's the fizz You're looking for I have these fruit-flavored carbonated water drinks." In response to Her rather skeptical look, I added, "They're sugar free even." The skepticism increased. "It helps me keep my figure." Yes, I know it was dumb; I

## The Forms of Things Unknown

didn't know what else to say. It's not every day that the Boss Lady drops by in person.

She sighed so deeply it sounded like something drawn from the bottom of the sea. "Well, I *suppose* you could make me a fizzy cocktail. Not that I need to watch my figure or anything."

Yikes! "Oh, goodness, I didn't mean to imply…"

She waved off my concerns with an airy gesture; I got to work on the cocktail. When I handed it to Her, She sniffed it as though trying to be sure it wasn't spoiled, then took a dainty but substantial sip. "This is terrible."

"I'm so sorry! If You like, I could…"

"Not necessary," She interrupted.

I finally broke the uncomfortable pause with, "I just learned to do that pretty recently, make drinks I mean, and I'm afraid I'm not very good at it yet."

"No, you're not. Luckily, neither your income nor your reputation depends on your skill at bartending."

"Yes. I mean no." I'm not easily tongue-tied, but there was more than ample cause. I would've been heartened by the fact that She had taken another sip, had it not been accompanied by a half-grimace. Time for another change of topic. "To what do I owe the great honor of this visit?"

Her smile lit up the room and instantly soothed the sting of Her previous comments. "Oh, I just happened to be in the neighborhood, and…" Now it was my turn to look incredulous, and She responded with a laugh so beautiful it virtually took my breath away. "No, I guess you won't believe that, will you?"

"Well, no, not really."

The smile became even lovelier. "I'm really very fond of you, you know." I was totally speechless. "Oh,

152

# Boss Lady

come now darling, surely you already knew that after all this time!"

"I…well…um…" Why was I crying?  Damn, so much for looking cool.

"I know that, since taking the job…how many years ago was it?"

"Twenty."  It came out sounding something like a croak.

"Twenty years!  How time flies!  Since taking the job twenty years ago, you've performed admirably and I really have noticed; it's just that I'm so very busy and, well, time gets away from one.  Sometimes I think of you and realize, 'Goodness, it's been years since I looked in on her!' and yet there you are, still faithfully toiling away at your mission as though I were breathing down your neck the whole time!"

"Thank you, My Lady; You know I always keep my promises."

"And so you have, dear girl.  I know I've been awful about keeping up with you; it's just this mood I've been in for the past 15 years or so.  And the reason I dropped by is to let you know that I'm going to try to do better."

I don't have a word to describe the complex mixture of emotions that boiled up in response, and I wouldn't have dared to vocalize it even if I had.  So I just sat there and sobbed like a schoolgirl, and She glided across the room to sit beside me and draw me into Her arms.  "There, there," She said, "It really will be all right.  I promise, by the Styx."
And then She kissed me, and if I live to be a hundred no kiss of mortal woman could ever hope to match that brief brush of Her lips against mine.

## The Forms of Things Unknown

I awoke with Her scent still all around me, and my face wet with tears. I had never had such an intensely real-seeming vision before, and it had thrown me off-balance; I felt like I needed to get up, collect my thoughts, get my jumbled emotions back in control and re-orient myself to consensual reality. I stumbled into the outer room, and my attention was immediately drawn to the vase of roses atop my desk; they seemed fresher than they had been, and of a deeper color and sweeter perfume than before. I gently, almost reverently stroked the petals of one, softer than a woman's skin, and then reached down to draw it from the vase so that I might examine it under better light. But in my fascination at the apparent revival of my flowers, I neglected to use caution in grasping the stem; the blood which welled forth from my finger was as red as the rose.

*Boss Lady*

# The Forms of Things Unknown

*Many people have remarked that my writing style is clearly influenced by the classic TV show,* The Twilight Zone: *the stories are short, tight, fantasies, sometimes creepy or unsettling, and often concluded with a twist ending. But that's not my only influence, and I'm sure you've noticed that when a story's debt to a specific author is particularly strong I acknowledge it in a note at the end. The next three stories weren't inspired by the works of any specific creator, but by entire genres; when I wrote this one I was thinking of old-time TV suspense dramas like* Alfred Hitchcock Presents.

# Double X

**A man can go from being a lover to being a stranger in three moves flat...but a woman under the guise of friendship will engage in acts of duplicity which come to light very much later.** - Anita Brookner

"We're going to have to move soon; I really think Eleanor is beginning to suspect."

"What makes you think that?" asked Hazel, handing him his drink and then moving behind him to rub his shoulders.

"Nothing I can really explain," he said, then after a sip: "When you've been married to somebody for twenty-seven years, you get to know all her little ways, and you notice when they change. You were married before, you know what I mean."

"Yes. But how do you know she isn't cheating on you, too?"

Ted laughed. "You don't know Eleanor; she's as cold a fish as there is. We were both virgins when we got married, and once we were done having kids she just wasn't interested any more. I've already told you this more than once."

"There's no need to get testy," she said reassuringly. "I just want you to consider all the possibilities so you don't start acting nervous and setting off *her* radar."

"Like I said, I think I already have. Oh, I've been very careful; before I met you I saw escorts for years, and before that I had cultivated a pattern of not really telling her much about my comings and goings. And since she leaves the money to me, it's always been easy to use as much as I

## The Forms of Things Unknown

want without her being the wiser. But lately, she's been requesting a lot more money for all sorts of things, as if she's trying to probe the state of our finances."

"Has she been questioning you or anything like that?"

"No, she wouldn't. Eleanor is maddeningly indirect; she never makes a statement when an insinuation will do, and whenever she's angry at me it always takes me days to figure out why. I'll never understand why so many women are like that; is it something on the X chromosome?"

"You have an X chromosome as well, Ted."

"I know, but maybe something on the Y cancels it out. Maybe real sneakiness requires a double X."

"Oh, *really*! Now you're just being ridiculous. I'm relatively straightforward, and you're *extremely* sneaky; if quietly converting most of your investments to negotiable form so you can fly off to Tahiti with your mistress doesn't qualify, I can't imagine what would."

Ted looked as though he had been slapped. "I'm not leaving her destitute," he said quietly; "In fact, as per your suggestion I transferred the house and several large investments into her name. I just want to divide the money fairly rather than leaving it to courts and lawyers who would probably give her everything."

"Oh, I'm sorry!" she said, hugging him closely. "I didn't mean to hurt you. It's just that I feel nervous, too, and dumb female stereotypes always get me irritated. Please forgive me."

"See, Hazel, this is what I'm talking about. You know how many women would apologize like you just did? Practically none. That's not a stereotype, it's just the truth; men usually end up having to apologize no matter who was wrong. I don't think you really understand how different you are from most women. I never believed I would fall in love

158

# *Double X*

with anyone ever again, much less want to live my life with her. But you just make me feel so special, so safe. I know I can trust you, and that we won't end up being strangers sleeping in the same bed like Eleanor and me."

"I promise you that will never happen," she said through glistening eyes. And then she kissed him, and for a while there was no more conversation.


A few days later, though, she brought up the subject again on the airplane. "I just can't help but feel guilty about what we did. I know the two of you really shouldn't have married in the first place, and that you haven't had a sex life in over 15 years. I know the kids are grown up, and we really do love each other, and there really wasn't a home to break up. But damn, don't you feel bad about running off with all the negotiables *as well as* the stuff he put in your name?"

Eleanor shrugged. "Not really. I left documents donating the house back to him, and he's still under fifty; he has twenty more years to build up again, and with no alimony that'll be easy with his salary. He'll be a lot better off in the long run than I would've been had he been the one to run off with you as he thought would happen."

"I suppose you're right," sighed Hazel. "But I still feel bad about playing him like I did."

"No worse than he thought he was playing me," Eleanor huffed. "He got what he deserved."

"Maybe," she replied. "But I guess he was right about women being the sneakier ones, after all."

# The Forms of Things Unknown

*The 1920s and '30s were the heyday of the pulps, cheaply-produced magazines crammed with new fiction in almost every genre imaginable. They were the forerunners of comic books and, in a way, of television and video games in that they provided affordable entertainment and tried to reach every possible niche market. Like their modern successors, they were often condemned by critics as lowbrow, but had a certain undeniable charm; many of the best tales are still read and anthologized today. This story was based on a dream I had on my first night in New Orleans at the end of my book tour for* Ladies of the Night; *perhaps it was inspired by a poster of sci-fi pulp covers Denise had on the wall of the guest room. Though modern science has rendered its setting highly dubious, I ask that you approach it as readers did those stories from nearly a century ago: as an imaginative tale of adventure on a fantastic world.*

# The Sum of Its Parts

Every time I looked up at that spectacular view of Saturn, I congratulated myself on having had the good sense to invest in topside property. Though it had meant a heavy mortgage, the expenditure of every penny I'd made my first year on Titan, and the calling-in of every favor I had accumulated, it was totally worth it; nearly every visitor to the colony preferred my club to the ones down in the red-light district, as did every local with any poetry in his soul. Sure, it meant I had to charge more for drinks and house fees, and to maintain a more discreet atmosphere than the anything-goes places in the backstreets. But you know what? I never liked working in that kind of place, and I'll be damned if my name was going to be attached to one. I could never have afforded the rent or the bribes to own a place this classy on Earth, but here it was still wide open for a gal with a little bit of business savvy and a lot of what Mama Nature gave her.

That's not to say that I didn't breathe a little sigh of relief every time I sat down with my books and saw loads more black ink than red. While it's true that there are few things more dependable than gents' desire for booze and female company when they're months away from population centers with a more even distribution of the sexes, it's also true that hospitality is always a precarious business and a proprietor always needs to be aware of developments that might queer the whole deal faster than sunset on Ceres. And on the particular night of which I'm about to tell you, one such development walked through my door and none-too-politely requested my company. Well, *demanded* is maybe a better word.

# The Forms of Things Unknown

Said development was about 190 centimeters tall, wore a badge and a blaster and looked a helluva lot like Fred McMurray; I mean the young *Double Indemnity* Fred McMurray, not the old Disney-comedy one. Which is kind of a funny coincidence, because I've often been told I look a lot like the young Barbara Stanwyck. By the time I excused myself from mingling and reached the office, he was looking through my file cabinet.

"Didn't your mama ever tell you it's not polite to riffle through a lady's drawers without her permission?" I asked from the doorway, projecting a nonchalance I did not feel.

"You're required to keep these available for inspection on demand; I'm demanding."

I shrugged. "Suit yourself. You'll find they're all in order; I pay my lawyer and my CPA to make sure they are. In fact, I could've delivered 'em to your office and saved you the trouble of coming all the way across town."

"I wanted to look the place over for myself. You know this sort of business isn't supposed to be operating on the surface; you appear to have been grandfathered in somehow, but I want you to know that I'll be watching, and if this place becomes a nuisance..."

I was sitting at the desk by this point. "Pleased to make your acquaintance too, Marshal," I said, blowing smoke in his direction before stubbing the cigarette out in the ashtray. "I get the feeling we'll be seeing a lot of each other."

"Count on it," he said, slamming the door on his way out. I will not record what I said the moment he was gone, because I don't want you to get the idea that I'm unladylike.

Though I learned long ago to keep control of my temper when dealing with men, I was boiling inside and

# The Sum of Its Parts

knew it would be a mistake to go back to the floor right then. So I left things in the capable hands of my assistant Frances, put on my thermal suit and decided to go for a walk along the lakeshore. Now, if you've never been to Titan (and let's face it, that's probably a safe assumption), I should probably explain that the lakes, rivers, swamps and seas here aren't made of water but of a liquid hydrocarbon mixture; it would probably smell like tar or gasoline, but since you need a helmet to go outside I can't be sure. If you absolutely have to know, ask a chemist. Anyhow, the native life seems to like it all right; the shallows of the lake swarm with bugs during the day, and even at night you can hear lots of things moving around in the water. Oil. Benzene? Oh, you know what I mean.

I was plenty mad when I left the dome, and by the time I had cooled off I had walked about three kilometers beyond the end of the well-travelled path. Not that I was worried, mind you; humans are by far the largest animals on Titan. The second-largest is a kind of giant slug massing about 30 kilos, and I suddenly realized I had walked right into the middle of a much larger aggregation of them than I'd ever seen or heard of. They like to lie in the mud sunning themselves during the day, in groups of maybe a few dozen at a time, but it was rare to see 'em at night. Yet here I was, surrounded by *hundreds* of the slimy things; though they are usually very shy and always flee the approach of humans by sliding into the lake, these weren't moving at all and I bet Doc Robinson would've given a month's pay to trade places with me right now because what had made me stop and wake up to my surroundings was nearly putting my foot in one.

# The Forms of Things Unknown

Doc could've saved his money, though, because I'd have gladly traded places with him for free. Yeah, they were harmless...but this was a much larger grouping than anybody had ever seen in one place, and at night to boot; it gave me the heebie-jeebies, and I decided that even the company of the new marshal would be preferable right now. But as I turned back, I realized that there was no place to go; the slugs had slithered onto the path behind me, and I couldn't move from the spot where I was standing without stepping on one. I don't scare easy, but let me plop you down alone on another planet, surrounded entirely by shapeless aliens, and let's see if you do any better than I did. I was totally terrified, and I guess I must've had my oxygen valve turned a bit too low for the combination of exertion and excitement because when they started closing in and actually *crawling up my legs* I passed out. Aw, who am I trying to kid? Like the heroine of a Victorian melodrama, I fainted.

By the time I opened my eyes again, my radiophone's readout said 23:14; I had only been out for maybe half an hour, but my surroundings were completely different and I shuddered when I realized the slugs must've dragged me here. I wasn't sure where "here" was, exactly, but it looked like a cave and the rocks were wet with slime. The entrance was above, so there was plenty enough Saturn-light for me to see that the group which had captured me was only a small fraction of the number here; there must have been thousands. Though I was still petrified they hadn't actually harmed me (except for the nice new grey hairs I had probably sprouted), and in fact were giving me a wide berth; the only bad thing was the unshakeable feeling that they were looking at me (despite the fact that they lack any visible sensory apparatus at all). After about ten minutes of calming myself, I decided to risk the radiophone; Frances answered.

# The Sum of Its Parts

"Hiya doll. Keeping things together over there?"

"Janet? Where in blazes are you? You've been gone for over two hours!"

"No time to explain now. Is Doc Robinson still there, and sober?"

"Yes and mostly. You want me to get him on the phone?"

"Please." The slugs hadn't moved; could they hear, or detect radio waves, or both? If so, they didn't seem overly concerned.

After several agonizing minutes, Doc came on the line; I was relieved that his speech was unslurred. "What can I do for you, my dear?"

"Doc, honey, what can you tell me about the slugs?"

"You mean the limaxomorphs? We don't know much about them yet; they spend most of their time submerged in the lakes, and don't do much of interest when they're basking. We've never even found remains to examine, but long-distance scans seem to indicate a very simple bodily structure, much lower on the evolutionary scale than the earthly gastropods they resemble."

"Could they be intelligent?"

"Mercy, no, dear girl; they don't seem to have anything like a brain that we can detect, though again we would need to dissect one to be sure. Still, we've never observed any behavior that would seem to indicate intelligence."

"How about coordinated group activity?"

"That's not really a sign of intelligence *per se*; ant and bee colonies have very sophisticated group behavior, but they're not intelligent as we understand the term."

# The Forms of Things Unknown

"So, abducting women wouldn't qualify?"

"Well, it depends; group hunting behaviors are not...wait, are you saying this isn't a theoretical question?"

"Not as such, no."

"They actually *abducted* you? When? How? Where are you now? What are they doing?"

"I'd call it dancing." While I had been talking, the slugs had seemed to become increasingly...well, *excited*, and sort of throbbed while swaying forward and backward. And just as the Doc started to ask those rapid-fire questions, they had begun to slowly slide sideways in a circle around me, not getting any closer. The ones who were not in direct proximity to me were still swaying and throbbing, as if to music I couldn't hear. And the weirdest part of the whole performance? I wasn't scared at all.

"*Dancing?*"

"I took a lot of lessons as a girl, Doc; dancing would be the word I'd use. Artistic expression through rhythmic movement."

"That still doesn't mean they're intelligent; birds do mating dances, for example."

"I don't think they want to mate with me, Doc; I think they're trying to communicate."

"What makes you think that?"

"Call it a hunch. I'm going to ring off now; I want to see how they react to that. But don't worry, I'll call as soon as something changes, and I'll answer if anyone calls me."

When I broke the connection, they abruptly stopped moving; they did not resume when I started talking to myself out loud, but did when I called the club again.

"Tell Doc they're sensitive to radio waves," I told Frances, then "I'll call when I learn anything else."

166

# The Sum of Its Parts

The slugs were still again for quite some time, and I began to get a bit thirsty. I hadn't intended to be gone so long, so I hadn't filled my water bottle; fortunately the air recirculator had recently been serviced, so I wouldn't suffocate unless I stayed here for several days. After a while I got up to stretch my legs; there was no reaction at all from my strange hosts. It was as though the only thing that excited them was electromagnetic energy.

That stray thought gave me an idea, so I activated my built-in torch and played the light over the slugs in the front row. The effect was almost immediate; they started to sway again for a few moments, then gorgeous ripples of color began to play over them as though someone were putting on a laser show. The colors changed, brightened and dimmed and moved in waves from slug to slug, not stopping for an instant when crossing between individuals, as though they were all part of a greater whole...Say, what if they were?

"Frances, put Doc on again...Doc, could all the slugs be one creature?"

"You mean like a bee colony, many creatures bound together in a swarm?"

"Sort of, only more so; what if the slugs aren't actually individuals at all, but simply cells connected together by telepathy or radio waves or something?" I explained how they had reacted to my light, and as I spoke they began to do their dance again while the colors ebbed and flowed among them in intricate patterns, like unearthly flowers blossoming and dying on shifting dunes, or like silent fireworks merged with rolling waves. It was the most beautiful thing I had ever seen in my entire life.

## The Forms of Things Unknown

"I think you may be onto something, my dear! If each limaxomorph is merely part of the greater whole...oh, my!"

"What?" I asked after a few moments of silence.

"They - or if we're right, it – may assume that we're connected to each other just as they are. Perhaps your abduction was, to it, nothing more than a tap on collective humanity's shoulder?"

"And the reason they – it – gets excited when I'm talking on the phone is that it believes I'm communicating to the rest of you like its cells communicate! Yes, that must be it! Doc, I'm going to try a few things here, so don't get worried if I'm quiet for a while."

"Understood."

I rang off, and though I expected it I couldn't help being disappointed when the color waves and dancing abruptly stopped. So I turned on the light again, and was rewarded with the colors; I called a friend I knew wasn't home, and the dance continued until her answering machine got tired of my talking nonsense and hung up on me. Then I stood up again, and started moving toward the entrance; the slugs didn't budge. Clearly, I wasn't going to get out of here until it was satisfied that we had understood whatever it was trying to say.

Sometime after one I fell asleep, but I didn't sleep well; I was haunted by nightmares of an immense, formless *something* peeling off my clothes and trying to get into my skull via my ears. Doc called once and Frances twice, and though the slug-collective responded as usual to the calls, it didn't do anything else.

If you've never slept in a spacesuit, I have some advice for you: Don't. They're not made for it, and you'll ache all over and be grumpy all the next day. So I was in

# The Sum of Its Parts

absolutely no mood to deal with the first phone call of the morning, Marshal McBusybody himself.

"What is going on, Miss Trevor? I called your office and they said you were out."

"You expected the owner of a nightclub to be awake at 0900?"

"Not really, but I heard that you left in a huff last night, never came back, and that Dr. Robinson spent the entire evening in your office."

"So you're spying on me, too? I don't think that's playing strictly by the rules, Marshal."

"You still haven't answered my question; what exactly is going on?"

"Ask your spies," I said, and hung up. Frances would get an earful from me later for letting him bully her into giving out my personal phone code. I had rather hoped that an angry conversation would cause a different reaction in the slugs, but no such luck; they reacted exactly the same way as before, and stopped when the call did. I tried explaining to them/it that I was hungry, exhausted, cramped and dying for a cigarette, and that I really despised having to take care of personal business in a spacesuit, but it was no use; I wasn't even sure they could hear me.

The morning dragged on, and though I tried everything from semaphore with my suit light to my best Ginger Rogers impression (or the closest to it I could get in space boots), the only reactions I got were the same ones I had before. Then at 10:37 I heard the amplified voice of my new adversary calling down from above, and the slugs didn't seem to like him any more than I did.

## The Forms of Things Unknown

"MISS TREVOR, THIS IS MARSHAL McBAIN. ARE YOU DOWN THERE?"

"Of course I'm down here, you imbecile! You obviously used a robohound to track me to this hole in the ground, so where did you think I'd be? In Detroit?"

"ARE YOU IN ANY IMMEDIATE DANGER?"

"If I were in immediate danger, I'd have been dead hours ago! Any more stupid questions?"

"WE'RE GOING TO LOWER YOU A LINE."

"You do that. Is Doc with you?"

"I'm here, dear girl!" he shouted down. "This is amazing; we had no idea there were this many of them in the area!"

"Yeah, well try to keep Captain Gungho there from killing 'em all until I get up there," I said as I adjusted the sling around my torso; "I think I know what they want."

Later in his office, I tried to drive my theory into the marshal's thick skull. "Look, it's not that complicated. If Doc and I are right, the slugs are one big creature. Not just in that lake, but all over Titan; your men found slime trails leading out in every direction from that cave. One single creature, spread out over a whole world."

"So?"

"So how do you think you'd feel if you were the only intelligent creature on a whole planet, with nobody else to talk to? And what if another creature came along that was so different from anything you knew, that you at first thought it wasn't intelligent, but then you realized it might be? Wouldn't you try to talk to it?"

"I suppose I would."

"Well of *course* you would, Marshal! And let's say it ignored your first few attempts..."

"What attempts?"

170

# The Sum of Its Parts

"Who knows? It could've been sending out all kinds of signals we didn't recognize as communication, right Doc?"

"Indubitably."

"Like he said. So wouldn't you eventually get frustrated and go to even greater lengths to attract the stranger's attention? Try to talk to her? To impress her with your charm and personality?"

"You think the slugs were *flirting* with you?" he asked incredulously, and with undisguised disgust.

"Not with me, Marshal, with us. It's one big organism, more than the sum of its parts, so naturally it thinks humanity is as well. Heck, maybe it's even right, in a way. But you seem to think loneliness is all about sex; it's not, you know. Not for slugs, and not for humans, either."

He looked at me for a long time before speaking. "Perhaps I misjudged you, Miss Trevor. You may be more of an asset to this colony than I had at first imagined."

"We all do that sometimes, Marshal; until last night, we thought the slugs were just mindless bottom-feeders. It takes a big person to admit he misjudged somebody or something."

For the first time since I'd met him, I saw a slight smile crack his face. "Well, I hope we still see a lot of each other."

I blew smoke in his direction and smiled back. "Count on it."

171

# The Forms of Things Unknown

*As I mentioned in the last introduction, the pulp magazines were one of the progenitors of comic books, which started out as essentially heavily-illustrated pulps. So I think it's fitting that a story inspired by the pulps be followed by one inspired by comic books: specifically, the horror comics of the 1970s that I grew up reading, such as* House of Mystery *and* The Witching Hour. *Those familiar with them will probably see the influence, but I hope even those who don't will enjoy the tale.*

# The Company of Strangers

"Daniel, unless you agree to see me more regularly, I honestly don't know how I'm going to help you. You not only refuse to come in every week, but to make regularly-scheduled appointments at all; I'm sure you realize that as long as you insist on only coming in when someone else has cancelled, our visits are going to be irregular and infrequent." The man she was addressing responded by getting up and walking to the window for the seventh time since the beginning of the session. "And would you *please* sit down?"

He complied, then looked around for his bottle of water and began to get up to fetch it; Dr. Nolan pre-empted the move by reaching for it herself, then leaning forward to give it to him. He drained the last of the water, sucking on the bottle for several seconds after it was dry as if to draw more water from the plastic, then replaced the cap and looked around for a wastebasket; the psychologist took the bottle from him so he wouldn't have the excuse to get up again. "I'm sorry, Doctor, but it has to be that way because of the nightmares."

"You mentioned them last time, but didn't elaborate; do they have anything to do with your inability to stick with a therapist for more than half a dozen visits?"

He nodded nervously, then leaned forward so his elbows rested on his knees and hung his head forward. "And with my inability to hold down a job, and with my refusal to set regular appointments," he said to the floor. "And it's why I don't live near my family and have no friends."

# The Forms of Things Unknown

"But surely your family hasn't abandoned you; our visits are billed to your father's insurance."

He continued to avoid eye contact, but responded, "No, it's not like that; my family loves me and I have plenty of friends who really want me to come home again. I know you probably don't believe this, but until these awful dreams started I never had any mental problems in my life."

"I believe that you believe it, Daniel, but recurring nightmares so disturbing they drive a person away from his family and friends don't spring out of nowhere. They come from some pre-existing issue that you've been unable or unwilling to acknowledge."

"I'll be damned if I know what that might be," he said, straightening up suddenly in the chair. "I can't remember any kind of childhood trauma, always did well in school, got along fine with everybody, graduated not all that far from the top of my class. The first person I had the dream about was my mother."

"Go on."

"I was living in an apartment, but you know how in dreams you're sometimes still living with your parents. Well, anyway, I don't even remember what I was doing in the dream, but my mother was in another room talking to me about something; it was just a regular conversation, nothing I can even recall. But when she came into the room, *she had no face!*"

"What do you mean, no face?"

"I mean exactly that, no fucking face! I mean the front of her head was totally smooth, no eyes or nose or mouth. And she just stood there with her head turned

# The Company of Strangers

toward me as though she was looking at me, only she had no eyes. And I woke up screaming."

She resisted the urge to ask him to sit down again; if pacing helped him unburden himself, so be it. "So you kept having this nightmare about your mother?"

"Not just about her. My dad, my little brother, my girlfriend, all of my friends, my boss...everybody I knew. Every damned night I had them. Every one was different; I would be doing some mundane thing, then without warning the other person in the dream would come into the room or turn around or whatever and have no face. And then I wake up."

"It never goes any further?"

"No, that's it, I always wake up as soon as I see that horrible faceless head."

"So why did you leave your home?"

"A few months after the nightmares started, my little brother went off to college. Then when he came home for a visit, I had the nightmare about him that very night. Thinking about it later, though, I realized that I hadn't dreamed of him even once while he was gone. I quit my job and went to work somewhere else...and my old boss immediately stopped appearing in the nightmares. It wasn't long after that I moved away."

"Did it help?"

"It worked perfectly. I only have the nightmare about people I know well, and even then only if I see them often. As long as I spend my days with strangers, my nights are peaceful. But if I get to know anyone too well, the nightmare comes back starring that person, except without a face."

## The Forms of Things Unknown

"So every time you get to know a therapist well..."

"...he or she starts appearing in the nightmare, and I have to stop going. Same thing with jobs; as soon as faceless versions of my boss or coworkers start haunting me, I quit. My neighbors probably think I'm a terrorist or something because I totally avoid talking to them, for fear of being forced to move. I'm hoping that if I see you sporadically, it will at least take longer for me to start having the dream about you."

"Well, at least I know what we're up against now. Please try to make another appointment as soon as you feel comfortable, and we'll see if we can't figure out the real reason you're so afraid to get close to anyone."

"Do you think that's what it is, Doctor Nolan?"

"I think it's very likely. Until then, try to keep your mind occupied, and try to at least call your family and friends if you can do that without setting off the nightmares."

After leaving her office, Daniel felt extremely agitated; talking about the problem had only served to churn up the terror in his mind, and despite the doctor's advice he didn't feel it wise to call home too often. A long walk in the park did nothing to clear his mind, nor did dinner and a movie, and he didn't like to go home between dinner and midnight because a couple of his neighbors often sat out on the steps talking on fine nights like this one. So he decided to seek some company from one of the girls who frequented the stroll about ten blocks from his place; the only one in sight when he arrived was a slender, 30-ish woman named Lisa he'd been with a few times before. It occurred to him that even seeing the same hooker too many times was probably not safe, but if he

176

# The Company of Strangers

started dreaming about any of them he'd just have to start going to massage parlors instead.

Lisa recognized him, and the deal was quickly made; he followed her to her room, and the two of them got undressed at the same time. He was still quite nervous from the afternoon's session, though, so he tried to focus on what she was doing so he'd get excited and forget about all that, at least for a little while. He watched as she kicked off her shoes, shimmied out of her dress, removed her underwear, and took off her face.

Only this time he didn't wake up.

# The Forms of Things Unknown

*This tale is quite short, and it's a good thing I had composed it in my mind prior to sitting down to write it, because that writing was finished only about an hour before I received the phone call telling me of Jae's accident.*

# Heat

She moved softly and silently along the branch, nearly invisible amidst the foliage; when it got too narrow to support her she dropped lightly down to the next tier, barely bending the lower branch as though she weighed nearly nothing. She stopped to sniff the air again and looked upwind, attempting to locate the source of the familiar-yet-strange odor, but she was not yet close enough; she therefore resumed her course along the branch, crossing effortlessly onto a limb of the next tree where the two intertwined.

After another half-hour of progress like this, punctuated by frequent stops to sniff the air or lie still when she heard a noise or sensed movement, she finally arrived at what her exquisitely-sensitive nose told her was her destination. It was a clearing like many others in the jungle, but this one was occupied by the creatures she had smelled from far away, the creatures who had aroused her appetite. But she was far too experienced a hunter to allow her hunger to cause her to act rashly; the prey were larger than she was, and she could not be sure that they could not seriously injure her. No, far better to stay on the branch above them for a while, silently lying in wait; sooner or later one of them would wander away from the others, and then she would strike from above without warning.

As she had anticipated, her opportunity eventually came; the majority of the group was occupied with something at the far end of the clearing, leaving one not only isolated, but cut off from the view of the others by a large, low shrub. Launching herself from the branch, she struck her quarry squarely between the shoulders, knocking him off of his feet. His scent was confusing; though it bore a strong

## The Forms of Things Unknown

resemblance to that of her own kind, it was somehow different and mingled with other peculiar odors. On top of that, his oddly-pale skin was covered with a strange layer of...hair? Hide? that seemed not to be a part of him. Fortunately, it was relatively fragile and easily ripped away, leaving him exposed for her purposes. It was all over in a few minutes, and though his cries attracted the attention of the others she was gone before they could arrive, moving through the trees like a will-o-the-wisp.

Later, around the campfire, Bennings mocked Grayson's story. "Come on, old man, 'fess up; you tore your khakis on that thorn bush after unwisely choosing it as a spot to relieve yourself. Surely you don't expect us to believe this ridiculous tale of your being raped by a wild woman!"

*Heat*

# The Forms of Things Unknown

*When I first published "Empathy" (which you can find in* Ladies of the Night) *on my blog, I was confronted in the comments by the dumbfounding realization that some otherwise-intelligent people do not understand that the protagonist of a story need not be good, morally-upright or even admirable in the author's eyes; she is merely the person the story follows, not some moral exemplar. Marilith is a courtesan on an Earth very different from the one we know, who has used her paranormal ability to excel in her profession and climb the social ladder. This tale takes place three years after the first, and if you haven't read that one yet* **I strongly** *suggest you do so; you may find it difficult to fully appreciate otherwise.*

# Willpower

Marilith's guest was ten minutes late, and even the aftereffects of the laudanum could not calm her agitation. It was not the disruption to her schedule that upset her so; Prince Jamal was her only client scheduled for the day, nor were any set for the next. The disquiet was at least partly due to the empathic focus she was struggling to maintain in the face of nearer, stronger voices, but the rest of it...

"Mistress, please," begged her handmaiden; "let me bring you something to calm you. I have never seen you in such a state."

"No!" snapped Marilith. "It's too late for that, Cynthia; he's long overdue already, and I'll need all my willpower for this. I've done all I can do, and now all that remains is to wait." As if in punctuation to her sentence, the soft gong which signified a new arrival on the landing stage sounded in the antechamber. And yet Cynthia hesitated with uncharacteristic inefficiency until her mistress ordered her to go.

The trip to the roof and back was not a long one, yet today it seemed interminable; by the time the Prince was announced, his hostess felt as though she was about to scream. But luckily for her, the emotional communication enabled by her psychic gift was unidirectional; he had no idea of the turmoil which raged behind her penetrating purple eyes and her soft, enigmatic smile. "Welcome back, Your Highness. It has been too long."

"Lies do not become you, Marilith," he said, and a wave of panic engulfed her; did he know what she was planning? How could he have discovered..."You would be just as happy if you never saw me again, except for the fact

# *The Forms of Things Unknown*

that you would then be cheated of the ridiculous fee I pay you."

"Your Highness does me an injustice; surely you don't believe I could hide such unkind thoughts without wearing them on my visage."

He laughed, an especially unpleasant laugh even by his standards. "You must think me a very great fool, woman; even a common whore knows how to disguise her true feelings for the men who pay her, and you are no common whore."

"As you say, My Lord. But if you believe this of me, perhaps you should find another courtesan more to your liking."

He pulled her up against him, and the wave of anger and hatred which engulfed her almost drowned her doubts and fears. "I would, if there were another fit to wash your feet," he said in a tone which weirdly mingled resentment with admiration; "besides, you know very well I couldn't trust anyone else."

"So you have said, My Lord," she said, suppressing a shudder as his right hand moved down from her waist, "but I fail to comprehend what makes me especially trustworthy. I can sense *your* feelings, not the other way around."

"You do more than just sense feelings, witch," he spat; "they become a part of you and overwhelm your own. I had prepared quite a dossier on you ere I approached you the first time; my advisors feel you would be incapable of violence because your victim's terror would overwhelm you."

"That is true, My Lord," she whispered in his ear, "but I am not the only one here."

Though she had experienced it many times, Marilith never failed to be astonished by the incredible silence with

# *Willpower*

which Cynthia could move when necessary. And though she had been fully apprised of her attendant's capabilities before she even purchased her, the reality was more terrifying than she could have dreamed. Two extra pairs of arms shot forth from her gown with the speed of striking cobras; six sets of razor-sharp fingernails glinted like gems for only an instant before they were coated in blood; thirty powerful digits ripped out the princely entrails with the ease and energy of a child scattering shredded paper from the interior of an eagerly-awaited package. And Marilith was not sure if she would ever stop screaming, much less sleep again. She drew her ornate dagger and plunged it into her servant's body over and over and over again; for her part Cynthia quietly accepted the attack, each wound closing instantly as though the blade had been plunged into water rather than flesh. And when the hysterical girl finally collapsed into wracking sobs and let the blade drop from her nerveless fingers, the dispassionate handmaiden gathered her up as gently as one might handle a sleeping kitten, and bore her toward the bath after stepping through the gore that had until recently been a human being.

Once she had pressed the prepared wine to her mistress' lips, bathed her tenderly and tucked her exhausted body into bed, Cynthia returned to scrub the carnage from the other room; she was unsurprised to find another man waiting there, surveying the scene with satisfaction. "So it's done?" he asked unnecessarily.

"As you see, Your Highness. My mistress' plan worked perfectly; she was able to remain focused on your emotions and thereby exclude Prince Jamal's, at least until I could strike. The kinsman who so troubled you is no more."

185

## The Forms of Things Unknown

"Good, very good. And my other operatives have informed me that all of his precautions have been foiled; he will not return this time."

"Forgive my boldness, Your Highness, but are you absolutely certain there is no chance my mistress will be implicated in this?"

"None whatever. Once you physically clean the area with the fluids you have been provided, my people will arrive before morning to remove the more intangible residues. If the investigators come here at all – which I doubt – they will find nothing."

"She has done you a great favor this evening, Mighty One."

"I am aware of that, Cynthia, and she will be handsomely rewarded as we agreed."

"You know that she will never be the same again."

"Indeed she will not; her patent of nobility is already in process, and once that's done it will be a small matter to negotiate an advantageous marriage for her."

"Thank you, Your Highness." Before she rose from the deep bow, the lifelike image had faded from view. And as she began the arduous process of cleaning, Cynthia thought to herself that though it might be disrespectful, she was very glad indeed that she was not human.

*Willpower*

# The Forms of Things Unknown

*One can never be sure exactly where inspiration will come from; I had the "knock knock knock" sound signifying text messages for over a year before this tale came to me late one night. The habit of texting friends when I'm high or drunk is also mine, I'm afraid, but that's where the similarity stops; I am much too cautious to partake unless I'm in a safe place with people I trust. That, however, would make for a very boring story, so...*

# Knock, Knock, Knock

Helen was a methodical sort of person; she believed in a place for everything and everything in its place. That's not to say she was stuffy; far from it. But her friends often gently teased her about the way she liked to have everything just so, and she had a system for everything it was possible to systematize. Take her phone, for example; every different alert was a distinctly different sound, so that she could know exactly what was happening and gauge whether to respond to it or not. The sound she had chosen for text messages was a knocking sound: a sharp *knock knock knock* meant a new text, and it was distinct enough that she could make it out even in a noisy environment.

Tonight, however, it wasn't noisy; in fact, the sound startled her in the quiet room where she was beginning to grow a bit drowsy over her book. She stole a look at the clock; 1:16 AM, which meant it was almost certainly Angela and she was almost certainly high as a kite. She picked up the phone; it was indeed her best friend.

*"hey baby wassup-thinking of u"*

Her finger flew quickly over the screen: *"Hi honey, having a good time tonight?"*

There was a longer-than-usual pause, then *knock knock knock*! *"Nah tonite sux, went out but evryplace was lame"*

*"So are you home safe?"*

Another really long pause, then finally *knock knock knock*! *"Not yet"*

*"So where are you?"*

The intervals between her texts and the replies were maddeningly-long tonight; usually Angela was quite a fast

## The Forms of Things Unknown

texter. But finally, after her screen had been dark for several minutes, it came again: *knock knock knock*! *"not sure"*

"*Not sure? WTF? How much have you had to drink?*"

Again the interminable interval, so she sent another one: "*Angela? Talk at me babe.*"

A short pause, then *knock knock knock*! *"Almost none just a crapy weak margarita*"

"*Then how can you not know where you are? Did some loser strand you somewhere?*"

She was just about to probe the silence with another text when *knock knock knock*! *"yah"*

"*Oh, damn, sweets, you need to stop dating these assholes. Why don't you just Uber home?*"

Almost ten minutes elapsed before the next *knock knock knock*! *"cant"*

Angela must've been much drunker than she was telling…maybe someone had drugged her drink? "*Honey, please ask somebody where you are or look at Google Maps and give me the address. I'll come get you.*"

It wasn't quite so long this time before the *knock knock knock*! *"no ill come there"*

Helen didn't like the idea of one of her friend's invariably-useless boyfriends having her address, but she was too worried at this point to care. "*Sure, baby, come on over.*"

There was no immediate acknowledgement, and Helen was just about to text again when the phone actually rang; it was the ringtone assigned to Angela's sister Leigh. "Hello, Leigh? Do you know where your sister is?"

The voice on the other end sounded strained and distorted. "Oh, Helen, I…I'm so sorry. I don't know how to tell you this…Angela's dead."

"That's not fucking funny, Leigh!"

190

# Knock, Knock, Knock

"Funny? Of course it isn't fucking funny! She was in a fucking wreck; the cops say her boyfriend was drunk!"

Helen felt as though her brain was numb. "Are...are you sure?"

"Yes I'm sure, I'm at the hospital now but there was nothing they could do. She was already dead when the paramedics got there."

"But...how long ago did this happen?"

"About an hour ago, maybe quarter after one." This time the long silence was on Helen's end. "Helen? Are you there?"

"Yeah, I...Leigh, some jerk has been texting me from Angela's phone; they must've picked it up right after the accident, or else she left it in a bar or something."

"What are you talking about? I have her phone right here. It was in her purse, and I think the battery's dead."

"You have...but...Leigh...I..."

*knock knock knock!*

"Helen? Sweetheart, if you want to come down here with me..."

*knock knock knock!*

"Helen, please say something! If you don't think you can drive I'll send Todd."

*knock knock knock!*

But Helen's voice was frozen in her throat, and the knocking wasn't coming from her phone.

# The Forms of Things Unknown

*If you read the foreword, I probably don't need to tell you the inspiration for this story. It was, I think, at least partly a kind of affirmation on my part: that she would not only pull through OK, but that things would somehow be the better in the long run for the catastrophe having happened.*

# Little Girl Found

**The most beautiful stories always start with wreckage.** –
Jack London

Lexi opened her eyes and gazed about at the
wreckage. Scratch that; she opened her *right* eye, because
despite her effort the left seemed unable to open. Indeed, the
entire left side of her body seemed to have been damaged in
the crash; her left leg seemed mostly all right, but her left arm
was stiff and weak, she thought she might be deaf in her left
ear, and she didn't want to think too hard about what the left
side of her head must look like.

On top of all that, she wasn't able to get up at all, and
wondered if something might be wrong with her back. A
little exploration with her right hand, however, revealed that
the problem was external; she was pinned down by a steel
beam across her midsection. Carefully, gingerly, she began
to inch her body backward, hoping to draw back far enough
that she could eventually sit up or roll over; she made just
enough progress to encourage her to continue, and after a
long series of adjustments she was finally clear enough to roll
up onto her right side in order to survey the situation more
thoroughly.

What she saw did nothing to ameliorate her concerns:
the ship was an utter shambles, and there was no sign of
motion from any other crew member beside herself. She
called out as best she could, but her voice sounded weak and
unfamiliar to her own ear; there was no response of any kind,
and after a few more tries she gave up and resumed her
efforts to extricate herself from the debris without help. Her
new position allowed her to reach a cable trunk, and pulling

# The Forms of Things Unknown

on it allowed her to make faster progress than mere inching; soon she was clear enough to sit up, and despite the near-uselessness of her left arm she was standing up a few minutes later.

Well, it was a reasonable approximation of standing, anyhow; "leaning on a bulkhead" would be a much more accurate analysis. But she was mostly vertical and mostly mobile, and that allowed her to move out of the storage bay in which she had been trapped; she soon found what she needed to patch up all the obvious damage to her body that her inexpert senses could locate, and then she limped up to the control deck. That wasn't much easier than pulling herself out of the wreckage had been; all the usual routes were blocked by jammed doors or fallen beams. But Lexi had a resourceful nature; she eventually made her way up a service crawlway, removing a panel to come up through the deck onto the bridge.

All that had come before was the easy part; Lexi was not a member of the bridge crew and therefore had no idea how to use any of the equipment there. But she could use a computer, so she knew she'd be able to eventually figure out how to activate the distress beacon even if the communications console proper were not functional. Here again she met obstacles: the main computer was nothing but junk, so she had to locate a functioning pocket model with the proper files, then locate those files and read as much of them as she could understand. With ship's power down she had to rig up the communications console to a portable power source; given that she had never been trained to do that task and only barely understood the principles involved, it was almost a miracle that she was finally able, after considerable effort, to bring the panel to life and activate the distress

# Little Girl Found

beacon. After that, it was just a matter of waiting; there wasn't much else she could do except sleep, so she did as much of that as she could while waiting for help to arrive.


"What a damned mess!" exclaimed Commander Norton. "Have they figured out yet how the distress beacon came on by itself after 17 days?"

"Yes, sir," said Lieutenant Baker, "but you're not going to believe it."

"Try me."

"Well, sir, the panel appears to have been manually rewired."

"On an unmanned ship?"

"Apparently, sir, the work was done by one of the land exploration units."

The older man glared at him. "Don't bullshit me, son."

"No bullshit, sir. Lieutenant Payne has worked extensively with the model, and she says their adaptive programming has often given rise to some pretty amazing results. Since they're designed to explore alien worlds alone, they need considerable ability to learn new information and skills in order to deal with unforeseen problems. Apparently, LE-XI was able to recognize that it was the only robot to survive the crash, and consulted a portable database for instructions on getting the beacon online again."

"That's hard to believe, even for adaptive programming."

"Lieutenant Payne said the same thing, sir; she said that LE-XI had demonstrated an unprecedented level of

# The Forms of Things Unknown

autonomous action, and she wondered if the crash might not have resulted in some serendipitous change to its brain function. The left side of its head is bashed in pretty badly, and if it hadn't awakened and offered a report upon our entry to the bridge, I would never have believed it was still functional."

They had been walking up the hull for most of the conversation, and had now reached the place where the salvage mission had cut through into the bridge. Baker's appraisal of the robot's condition had been generous: there was a dent in its head the size of a large man's hand, and the sensory apparatus on that side was smashed. Its left arm was bent so badly its left hand wasn't far from the elbow, and its torso was in terrible shape. But its head swiveled crookedly on its neck assembly when the commander entered, and its remaining eye focused on him when he spoke.

"So this is the robot who saved the mission?"

"Yes, sir," said Lt. Payne. "LE-XI managed to exceed her programming remarkably. Lexi, this is Commander Norton."

"I'm very pleased to meet you, Commander; I hope I performed adequately." The robot's voice unit had also been damaged, so that instead of the clear mezzo-soprano it was designed to produce a childlike soprano emerged. Norton had always felt a bit silly talking to robots as though they could actually think, but in this case the illusion of personality was extremely strong.

"More than adequately, Lexi. Your actions allowed us to recover the data and samples you and the others collected here." Norton ignored Payne's ill-disguised grin; in spite of himself, he did feel gratitude and even a bit of admiration toward the damaged machine.

196

# Little Girl Found

"And what's more, Lexi," Payne added excitedly, "we're going to take you back to Earth to figure out how you did it, and maybe we can build more robots as smart as you are. I'm going to shut you down now for the trip, is that OK?"

"Yes ma'am, whatever you say," Lexi replied, satisfied in her way that she had pleased her makers and looking forward to the prospect of a long and restful sleep.

# The Forms of Things Unknown

*This is definitely the most Christmassy of the three Christmas stories in this book; in fact, I hope you don't find it too sweet and sentimental. If it seems lacking in depth, you might amuse yourself by wondering why I made it a period piece, and what significance (if any) this particular time period has to the story.*

# Christmas Cookie

Reggie opened the door to a sight he hadn't quite expected. Oh, she was as pretty as she had represented herself to be, and probably not too much older than she had claimed on the phone. But she hadn't warned him that her hair was so *shockingly* red, and somehow he'd figured she would dress a bit more…conservatively.

"Ho ho ho," she said with a rather silly grin.

"That's not funny," he replied, then "get in here before the neighbors see you."

"Wow, what a Grinch," she said, dusting the snow off of her fur-trimmed red coat. "What did you expect when you hired a hooker named Holly on Christmas Eve?"

"The agency's ad said 'discreet'."

"Trust me, honey, I didn't stand around on your porch any longer than I had to. And unless you've got lots of sweet young things coming in and out of here for other reasons, I sincerely doubt my seasonal getup raised any more eyebrows than my just being here in the first place did."

"Yeah, I guess you're right; I've just never done this before." In response to her skeptical look, he added, "Had a girl come to my house, I mean."

"Ah. Well, I don't need to ask why you decided to start tonight."

"What do you mean?"

"Lots of unmarried men call on holidays; it's tough being alone when the entire culture is loudly extolling the joys of family for weeks on end."

"You're pretty smart."

## The Forms of Things Unknown

She shrugged. "Not smart enough to make grad school easy. Hey, do you have anything hot to drink? This outfit isn't as warm as it looks."

"Nothing ready, but we could make something in the kitchen."

"Bitchin'. You got any cocoa?"

"I think I have some of the instant kind."

She rolled her eyes. "It'll have to do." Then after looking around for a few moments: "Don't you have a kettle?"

"You can heat up the water in the microwave oven."

"Nah, I don't trust those things. My mom got one last year, but I'm kind of afraid they might cause cancer."

"Suit yourself," he said, handing her a pot from the cupboard.

"Will you have some with me? I brought cookies."

He laughed in spite of himself. "You're quite a character."

"So they tell me. Gingerbread or sugar?"

A few minutes later, they sat at the table, drinking cocoa and eating cookies; at some point she had deftly made the cash envelope disappear. And before too long he found himself telling her about the divorce, and the increasing pressures of work, and the sense of loss and loneliness he had hoped to dispel this evening in some way that didn't involve drinking himself unconscious. The eventual move to the sofa was very natural, and for some reason he was completely unsurprised when she pulled a VHS copy of *It's a Wonderful Life* out of her absurdly-large purse and suggested they watch it together.

When she finally dressed to go, it didn't bother him at all that they hadn't done what he thought he wanted to do when he opened the phone book; in fact, he was so happy

# Christmas Cookie

with her that he pressed an extra $50 bill into her hand. She gave him a very warm and sincere hug, and as she opened the door to leave he could hear the bells of the nearby church signaling the beginning of midnight mass.

"Every time a bell rings…" she said, laughing.

He laughed with her, and then said, almost as an afterthought, "You never did tell me what you're studying."

"Psychology," she replied, almost sheepishly.

"But of course. Thank you, Holly; you were wonderful."

"You're welcome. Merry Christmas, Reggie, and a very Happy New Year!"

"I'm certain now that it will be. I'll call you again soon."

"I hope so!" And then she danced across the lawn, stopping to catch a snowflake on her tongue before waving to him from the gate and disappearing into a night that now seemed far less cold to him than it had a few hours before.

# The Forms of Things Unknown

*If you've never read either my blog or* Ladies of the Night, *you may be unfamiliar with Aella the Amazon; if so, this story (and the two following it) will make little sense to you unless you first read "A Decent Boldness", "A Haughty Spirit" and "Glorious Gifts", all of which appear in* Ladies. *If you've already read them and you're the kind of person who pays attention to such things, you probably noticed that all three of those stories were written in the present progressive tense, without dialogue; in other words, we experience the story just as Aella does in her head, as it happens. This one is different, and though the next returns to the familiar pattern, the one after that...well, you'll see.*

# Wise To Resolve

**Wise to resolve, and patient to perform.** -
Homer, *Odyssey* (IV, 372)

To My Dearest Friend Phaedra,
May Tethys Protect and Enrich Thee:

  I pray this letter finds thee well, and that thou wilt
forgive my poor grammar and worse penmanship. I have
written it in Tarshi because it is of the utmost importance that
its contents are kept a secret between us, and I know that no
one in my country and few in thine can read it. My people
already believe me to have become somewhat erratic due to
my years spent in Man's World, and I fear if they knew what I
was planning I might not escape as easily as I did that
unpleasantness about the spring festival six years ago.
  Thou wilt remember that I conceived by the wealthy
Scythian who gifted me with the beautiful kine, and bore a
healthy son; thou wilt also remember that by the ancient pact
between their people and ours, sons go to live with their
fathers while we keep the daughters. Most of my people see a
son as no more than bad luck, a necessary but unfortunate side
effect of the lottery which might also produce a daughter. But
somehow I could not be quite so unconcerned; even in the
three months between his birth and the Spring Festival I had
become very attached to him, and though I spoke it not aloud I
gave him a secret name in my heart, Asterios. I suppose my
Aunt Laomache is right, and I have been contaminated by
outlandish ideas; I've known so many good men, both in
Tartessos and during the months I spent at thy mother's in
Knossos, that I can no longer think of them merely as a

# The Forms of Things Unknown

necessary evil (no matter how bad most of them may be). Furthermore, his father Niall and I have mated every year since at the festival, and he always makes me a present of more kine; I thus see my son (whom his father named Hemek) every spring, and again on the occasions when our clans have met for trading after harvest, and every day (or so I fancy) in the faces of the two daughters I have borne since, who strongly resemble their brother.

So though it is not considered proper among my people to care about the fates of sons, the heart cannot be commanded by mortal woman. I know not why I feel such a powerful concern for his health and happiness, but feel it I do, and I have come to the conclusion that it is wrong to deny him the advantages his sisters will have. The Scythians are great warriors and horsemen, but they are not civilized like we Amazons; they spend most of the year roaming the steppes, living in tents and grazing their herds hither and yon. They have no writing and little in the way of art, and even their music and poetry are crude. So though my son is already strong and skilled for his five years, I want more for him than to be a mere herdsman. If wandering be the way of his father's people, so be it, but let him wander among the cities of the West rather than the endless seas of grass in the East. Let him go forth and learn about all the wonders of the world as I have, and come home a wealthy, important and learned man, perhaps one able to bring culture to his noble but naïve race.

I have spoken to Niall about this, and we are in agreement; he is very impressed with the knowledge I gained in my travels, and he would like his son to have similar learning. If it meet with thy approval, we will send Hemek to thee two springs hence with the same captain who bears this letter; in the years I have known him I have found him to be an honorable man, and I believe I can trust him to deliver the boy

# Wise To Resolve

safely into thy keeping in Knossos. I also know thou hast important kin who can secure the necessary seals and papers to doubly insure that he not be abused or sold into slavery before he reaches thy house. I charge thee to love him as thou lovest me, and to rear and educate him alongside thine own son; once I receive confirmation of his safe passage I will also pay the same captain to carry thee a sum of gold sufficient to pay whatever sum his teachers demand, and a like sum every year until his education should be complete.

Though I am a loyal Amazon and love my family and my mother country, I am no longer the pigheaded provincial I was when we met so long ago; I have learned that there are many ways for men and women to relate to one another, and have grown wise enough to understand that our ways are not necessarily the best. Legend says our first queen established our laws so that we would never be dominated by men, and while I saw the kind of society she wished to avoid in several of the places we visited, in Crete I saw men and women living together as equals. Perhaps thy people are morally superior to all others, yet I know them to be just as mortal; I therefore assume this to be the result of superior teaching and wiser laws. That is the other reason I wish my son to be educated there; perhaps he can bring that wisdom back to his father's people, and his mother's people can in turn learn from them. I do not believe that even a son of mine can create a new Golden Age singlehandedly, nor that such a thing is even possible. But if change is to happen it has to start somewhere, and who better to start it than one of Amazon blood?

With Sincere Love and Gratitude, Thine Own True Friend Always, Aella

# The Forms of Things Unknown

*When June, 2015 arrived I honestly didn't think I had another story of Aella in me, but as I pondered what I would write instead, I happened to look up from my desk and lo and behold, there she was across the room from me – sitting on the divan, leaning on her sword with her cloak of honor about her shoulders, and dripping rain from the storms of centuries upon my rug. "Stop dallying, girl," she said to me, "hasten thou to write down my story for all who have ears to hear." When I indignantly replied that I was no girl but a full-grown woman of as many years as she, the reply came, "I lived and died over five thousand years before thy mother's mother was born, thou soft-handed tart, and no daughter of Pandora with as few scars as thou hast would be counted as a grown woman amongst my people." Far be it from me to argue with an ancestor who had come so far to pay me a visit, so here is her story just as she told it to me, minus the outlandish profanity.*

# The Generation of Leaves

**As is the generation of leaves, so is that of humanity.**
**The wind scatters the leaves on the ground, but the live timber**
**Burgeons with leaves again in the season of spring returning.**
– Homer, *Iliad* (VI, 146-149)

Eurynome teach these young girls their manners!

Oh, they pretend to be deferential enough; it's all "Honored One" and "General" and "Good Dame" out loud, but I see the impatience in their eyes and the half-hidden smiles as I strap on my sword, don my cloak and place my helm upon my head. I can almost hear their thoughts; they believe that no matter what my prowess in directing troops may be, I am too old and battle-weary to make good account of myself in personal combat any longer. But that is because they are too wet behind the ears to understand that age and wisdom will always overcome youth and strength, and one day perhaps I'll have to show them by knocking one flat on her pretty face.

And what's so important about this reception, anyway? It's not as though I haven't met a hundred merchants seeking to trade in our land since I was appointed Keeper of the Port. And it's not as though this is anything other than a mere formality; a captain who couldn't present the proper papers or other tokens of good faith would already have been turned away without an important official having to go out in the rain. It's just a lot of damned foolish ceremony; give me a good honest battle any day, and Hecate take all this rigmarole. Well, at least I have a chariot with an

207

# The Forms of Things Unknown

awning, while my impatient bodyguard are forced to sit on horseback exposed to the weather; age and rank do carry some privileges, after all, though the price be aching joints and poor sleep. And at least the road to the wharf is paved, so there is no chance of my conveyance becoming stuck and delaying my return home in time for luncheon.

How now, what's this? The ship bears the painted sails of Crete, whence none have come since before the last war made our waters more dangerous than they cared to brave. Dare I hope this ship will bear a letter from my dearest friend Phaedra, whose face I have not seen since before my young attendants were born? Would that it were so! To read her words and hold in my hand papyrus that she had sealed with her own would be the next best thing to kissing her again and feeling my heart lifted by the sound of her voice. Already I can see the multicolored skirts of a Cretan woman, standing on the quay beside a tall young man; perhaps she bears the letter I have longed to see for so many years. As I approach I see that she is hooded against the rain, and bears a bundle beneath her cloak; perhaps it contains precious papyri that she cannot risk getting wet?

Now my chariot stops, and I hear a hubbub among the guards; it seems that the young man has specifically asked to meet me, by name rather than by my title of office. By all the goddesses, can I dare hope? Though I have never laid eyes upon him before, his visage is familiar, and though he wears the clothing of a man of Crete, he speaks haltingly in the Amazon tongue as one might who had not used it in many years. And when the guards announce my arrival, his face beams and his voice breaks with emotion as he calls me his mother. Some of the bystanders laugh, others seem shocked or even offended; for no Amazon claims her sons

208

## The Generation of Leaves

after she hands them over to their Scythian sires, and no Scythian man would be foolish enough to expect his Amazon mother to acknowledge him. But all of their voices grow silent as I step forward to embrace him, and the soft rain from Heaven disguises the tears upon my cheeks as he introduces his wife and places my infant granddaughter in my arms.

# The Forms of Things Unknown

*This is one of those peculiar line-smudging moments I
warned you about at the beginning of the book; of course it's
a sequel to "The Generation of Leaves", but it's also a
sequel to the introduction to that story, and in a very real way
to "Boss Lady". It also smudges lines in a different way than
that. Events in the past for which we have records are called
"history", and those for which we don't are called
"legends"; those which involve goddesses and enchantment
and things of which we have neither record nor relic are
called "myths". But there are parts of the past in which
those three overlap, and sometimes – as Schliemann proved –
things that were thought pure myth may actually have existed
in some form in history, and beings thought to be purely
mythical might have very human kin living among us.*

210

# None of Woman Born

**None of woman born, coward or brave, can shun his destiny.** – Homer, *Iliad* (III, 120-121)

Since I live alone, it was both startling and disorienting to be roused roughly from sleep by someone shaking me. But when in response to my groggy queries, I heard a less-than-familiar voice say, "Wake up girl, for I have need of thee," I sat bolt upright and strained my eyes to make out the figure looming over my bed in the dark. The meager light filtering in from the front windows glinted upon metal, and I soon realized my nocturnal visitor was clad in ornate armor; she carried a helm under her arm and a sword with jeweled hilt hung at her side.

"Aella?" I asked.

"Show some respect, child," she said gently. "Though I am not wont to stand on ceremony, it would behoove thee to address an honored ancestor with something more than her common name."

"I'm sorry," I mumbled; "you did wake me up from a rather sound sleep. Would 'grandmother' do? We'll be here all night if I have to list all the 'greats' which should precede it."

She laughed, a strong but weary laugh that seemed to come from someplace deep inside her. "Aye, it will do. Dost thou always awaken so sluggishly? What if enemies attacked in the night?"

"It would make little difference; my enemies are cowards who always attack with overwhelming force. They fear a fair fight."

## The Forms of Things Unknown

She was not impressed. "Any descendant of mine should be ready to at least give a good account of herself in battle. Her enemies should long remember how dear a price they paid for their victory over her."

"I'm sorry, honored grandmother. Though I am a warrior in my own right, I'm afraid you would not recognize my battlefield as such."

"So I am told. Yet thou hast shown tremendous courage."

"Well, that's what some people call it. It's really just tremendous stubbornness."

She laughed again. "Then it is certain thou art of my blood, for my excess of pigheadedness was also lauded as courage both in my day and after it."

"I've wanted to ask you about that for some time, but you're not exactly easy to reach. I'm guessing the legends about Amazons and Scythians settling in Galicia have a basis in fact?"

"Aye. My son and his wife were unable to adapt to Amazon culture, and I was unwilling to let them return to Crete knowing full well I might never see them again. So I recruited a group of colonists, Amazons and Scythians both, and we sailed toward the setting sun and settled north of Tartessos."

"I seem to remember that you hated sailing."

She shrugged. "One does what one must."

"Yes. We all need to do things we hate and fear to accomplish the goals that are important to us."

"Aye, child, that we do. But make not the foolish error I did, of thinking that thy destiny is thine to command. Thou hast a task to perform, and thy course was charted for thee by the blessed goddesses long before thy birth, even as mine was.

212

# None of Woman Born

We are but the tools by which they accomplish their goals, which are not for the likes of us to divine."

I replied quietly, "I like to think I have free will."

She laughed once more, a soft chuckle tinged with pain. "I, too, enjoyed that belief."

"And what of Phaedra?" I asked, trying to change the subject. "Did you ever see her again?"

"Nothing could have stopped me save the goddesses themselves; had I been told she was dead I would have battled my way down to the Styx to find her. Her ships carried our colonists forth, and kept us supplied until my death."

"I reckon loyalty runs in our bloodline, too." She nodded. "Honored Grandmother, you said you were here tonight because you had need of me."

"Ah, that. Well, truth be told, child, I'm here because *thou* hast need of *me*."

"Oh. Will the coming years be that difficult?"

"I am no soothsayer, granddaughter; I know not what lies in store for thee. I know only that I was sent to remind thee of who and what thou art, to admonish thee not to forget the warrior blood that runs strong in thy veins, and to tell thee that though I lack the wisdom and learning to understand thy struggle, I am filled with pride for thy steadfastness and refusal to surrender. Thou hast done well, and I am certain thou wilt continue to do so. Because if thou shouldst dishonor my legacy by cowardice, I swear by our common ancestresses that I will return and beat thee to within a hairsbreadth of thy life."

"Thank you, grandmother. I think." She smiled, and laid her hand upon my shoulder, and then she was gone, leaving behind nothing but the weight of her millennia-long shadow upon me.

# The Forms of Things Unknown

*These last two tales are, in my mind, rather flawed. My own opinion of this one is that it's much too didactic, and I was going to leave it out of the book. But when I sent a preliminary draft to Chester Brown so he could find inspiration for his beautiful cover art, he specifically asked about this tale and requested that I include it. So if you like it, you have Chester to thank for it being here; if you don't, I'm afraid I have to bear the blame for writing it.*

214

# Travelers' Tales

**This world of imagination is the world of eternity.** –
William Blake

     In a place that is not a place as material beings
understand the term, on a plane of existence several levels
above our own, three friends came together to share stories of
their travels since the last time they had met.  I shall refer to
them as Red, Green and Blue, but what they actually call
themselves (if indeed they use a concept as crude as "name")
I do not know.  As was their custom they eventually lapsed
into a philosophical discussion, debating various ideas in
much the same way as sentient beings everywhere in the
multiverse do, and one of the topics they touched upon was
the ephemeral nature of the societies created by material
beings.  Soon the conversation turned to a comparison of
these societies, and they began to speculate about which of
these had the lowest likelihood of still existing in a
recognizable form by the time they got around to visiting it
again.

     "I visited a world whose inhabitants were expending
its resources at a shocking rate," ventured Red.  "They had
developed technological means of improving their physical
conditions, but made not the slightest effort to calculate the
probable supply of the raw materials consumed in the
process, nor even the most basic contingency plans for the
eventual depletion of those materials.  Though enough of
them were skilled in the development and use of technology
to maintain and even improve their control over their
environment, the majority of the population was fixated on
an irrational belief system which pretended that beings from

215

## *The Forms of Things Unknown*

higher planes like ourselves had nothing better to do than to watch over them constantly, protecting them from the consequences of their own foolish actions. Though they believed such beings could transcend the laws of nature and violate conservation of energy, they simultaneously imagined that the beings were obsessed with the tiniest details of their behavior, and would dole out reward or punishment based upon how closely each individual could adhere to a set of arbitrary, pointless and mutually contradictory rules. So rather than prepare themselves for the ultimate necessity of modifying their procedures to maintain or improve their current standards of living, they instead devoted tremendous effort to asking nonexistent benefactors to somehow materialize favorable consequences for them, and to spying on each other to ensure nobody was breaking any of the silly rules which they imagined their incorporeal benefactors to care about above all else.

"Surely, such a misguided sense of priorities must eventually result in catastrophe; if they fail to think ahead they must eventually reach a point where their resources run out, and when that happens their society must either collapse or decline into barbarism."

"That is indeed a sorry situation," replied Green, "but I think we must all agree that whatever the chances of such a civilization's survival, they would be lower still if those hapless creatures were burdened with even more deficiencies. I visited a world very like the one you just described, but in addition to the resource depletion, irrational belief system and refusal to face reality, they were also incredibly violent. A large fraction of their already-limited means was expended in the infliction of harm upon one another, and when they could find no sensible reason to do so they invented ridiculous ones. Like the beings you visited, they were obsessed with monitoring each others' mindless obedience to foolish regulations, but they further believed that they had the right to inflict violence upon each other for even the smallest and most inconsequential violations of those regulations. They even selected from among their number a designated group whose entire purpose was to go about not only looking for rule-breaking, but to actually deceive their fellows into breaking rules so as to provide an excuse for the infliction of violence. Nor was this violence limited by some principle of proportionality; these special agents were allowed to inflict grievous, even fatal harm upon their victims for even the tiniest transgression of the most obscure rule. And when they could not discover a large enough number of rule-breakers to satisfy their assigned quotas, they would simply pick victims at random, falsely accuse them and inflict harm just as though they had actually done whatever it was they were accused of."

"Incredible!" rejoined Red.

"There's more. Though there were already so many rules it was totally impossible for any of them to ever learn them all, they designated another group whose entire function was to invent *even more* of them, and to ensure they were too complicated for the ordinary individual to understand; they were written in a form of code so that none without special training could even hope to comprehend them. And if these rule-makers failed to make enough new rules to satisfy certain other individuals, they were criticized for inefficiency.

"It seems inconceivable that such a civilization could even last long enough to run out of resources; surely they must destroy themselves well before that point."

## The Forms of Things Unknown

But then it was Blue's turn. "I fear that the world I visited must come to a bad end even more quickly still, for its inhabitants were afflicted by all of the behavioral flaws the two of you have described, and another which I consider still worse. Like many material life-forms, they reproduced sexually and the biological drive to mate was a strong one. But though the act of reproductive union was so pleasant to them that they would use every opportunity to engage in it, even when biological conditions did not allow impregnation, they simultaneously believed that the act rendered them ritually impure. A very large fraction of their arbitrary rules were dedicated to restricting the act of mating, and infractions of these rules were held to be among the most serious of all, and subject to some of the harshest penalties in the society. Furthermore, mated pairs were supposed to be exclusive despite the fact that one of the biological sexes tended to have a much stronger and less selective drive than the other, and though transgressions against that exclusivity were extremely common they all pretended that their own mates would never behave so. An entire profession was dedicated to allowing the expenditure of such urges in a controlled fashion so as to reduce the potential harm resulting from transgressive mating; without this profession the long-term pair-bonding upon which their entire social structure was built would undoubtedly fail far more often than it did. Yet those who practiced it were vilified and stigmatized by most of their societies, even by those who used their services, and the rule-enforcers spent wildly disproportionate amounts of time and effort in their persecution. Furthermore, they seemed to labor under the delusion that if they could only cage everyone they discovered in this transaction, the biological basis for it would vanish without affecting their rate of population replacement.

218

# *Travelers' Tales*

"Given that such a large fraction of their racial energies was expended upon a wholly futile task which, if they could somehow succeed at it, would totally destroy the foundations of their society, I cannot believe that this culture still exists in the form I perceived it. Such mass derangement must surely prove disastrous within a relatively small number of generations."

The friends agreed that the world Blue had visited must indeed have fallen into chaos by now, and was therefore the worst of all those they had seen. Perhaps they were wrong; it may be that as astral entities they had an imperfect understanding of the tenacity and adaptability of material life. Or perhaps the time-scale on which they functioned was so protracted that nearly any society of material beings would perish quickly by their standards; it may be that "soon" to them would be twice ten thousand years by the way we measure time. Conversely, it may be that my poor, ephemeral brain of matter was unable to grasp the true nature of their conversation, and that upon awakening from this vision I filled in the gaps with my own mortal preoccupations. And really, in all likelihood, Red, Green and Blue exist only in my imagination (and now in yours), and this entire tale is but the idle fancy of a tired and cynical mind.

We'd better hope so, anyway.

# The Forms of Things Unknown

*This story bears much in common with a number of others in this volume. Like some, it was written long before I started sex work (1993 in this case), and like some it was inspired by a dream. But it's remarkable in two ways: it's the only story I ever wrote on a bet, and it's the only one I've ever written in first-person male voice. In the original dream, I was the character I've named "Carol", but as you will see she exits the stage pretty quickly (at which point I woke up). So when I was talking to my first husband Jack about it the next day, I pointed out that if I were to turn it into a story I'd have to do it from the hero's point of view. He scoffed at the idea that I could write convincingly from a male POV, which of course irritated me and I bet him I could. This was the result; Jack agreed it was a good story, though he would not concede the bet because he said I made one pretty glaring error in male psychology. I was only 26 at the time, so naturally I huffed and pouted and told him he was wrong. But male friends who've read the story since have all pointed out the same lapse. So OK, Jack, I'll give you that one. I still think it's a fun story, though, and I hope you do too, dear reader.*

# Eight Minute Warning

Short-range precognition isn't the most versatile psionic ability to be born with. It certainly doesn't help your love life (what woman could stand a man who knows just what she plans to do eight minutes before she does it?), and it makes you *persona non grata* at every racetrack and casino in the galaxy. It will, however, make you one hell of a tactical officer, which is exactly where it landed me. Even a few seconds of early warning can make all of the difference in a hyperspace dogfight, and after I had provided the early warnings that turned a dozen or so battles around, I was kicked up the promotions ladder to full commander and posted to space station GO-342, the command post for one of the most volatile sectors of the galaxy.

Not that I'm complaining, mind you. Even though it meant kissing wife #5 bye-bye, the combination of deep space pay, hazardous duty pay, and special ability bonus, plus the perks that come with moving in the rarefied atmosphere of the upper command structure, made the move very worthwhile and put me on the fast track to getting my own ship or station. I really wish the opportunity to win that command hadn't happened in quite the way it did, however - for a while there I wasn't sure if I'd even live to my next paycheck, much less see a fat raise added to it.

Like all truly bizarre incidents, this one started innocuously enough - in the station's artificial swimming lake, complete with beach and sun. I was having a little swim, enjoying off-duty hours, when suddenly that funny feeling came over me - the *deja-vu* like realization of what was about to happen. As always, happen it did, this time in the person of Carol McCormac. My command of the English

## The Forms of Things Unknown

language is woefully inadequate to properly describe Carol, but for the sake of continuity I'll try. First off, imagine this beautiful head of perfect blond hair that falls just the right way and never seems to need to be arranged with any more effort than a toss of the head. Add to that piercing green eyes, silky skin the color of milk, a soft and musical voice, and a set of knockers that she can barely reach around, and you'll just begin to get the picture. Best of all, she's always been crazy about me and vice versa. I met her between wives #3 and #4, and it didn't take me long to realize that I was in love. No matter how hard I tried, though, Carol always avoided getting serious with me. I think it was because she had some ridiculous idea that her rather unsavory personal sexual history made her not good enough for me. What a laugh.

Right away, though, I sensed that this time was going to be different, and it wasn't just because she was wearing a topless bathing suit. Every time we met like this after a long separation, our eyes would lock and we would just sort of stand there and stare at one another for awhile, but this time there was an extra element between us, a force as palpable as electricity and a whole lot more comfortable to be hit by. Had I not been waist-deep in water I would have run up to her, but I still did a pretty good simulation of it. I swept her into my arms and she assumed that peculiar sideways position that her bustline required and leaned back to be kissed.

After a few minutes of that she looked up at me with a cozy expression and said, "Hi."

Not one to be outdone in nonchalance, I replied with "Why don't we get married?"

"Ooh, you're starting in quick this time," she said with a slight frown. "You know I can't marry you."

222

# Eight Minute Warning

"We've been over this a thousand times, baby. Why the hell not?"

"It's because of my past, you know that. It wouldn't look good for an officer to marry someone who..." she trailed off, as she always did at this point in the argument.

"It can't look any worse than being married five times, and they didn't hire me for my morals. Besides, my second wife was a prostitute before I met her."

"*Really?*" she asked, with a kind of innocent incredulity that made me want to kiss her again; I saw my opening, however, and refrained so I could go for the jugular.

"Really. And it didn't bother me one bit."

"Then how come you're not still married to her?"

Ooh, good counter. "Let's just say she was unable to put her work behind her. You're different, though. I could never believe you'd act that way."

She could see I truly meant it. "We'll talk about it later," she said. "Right now, I want to go someplace more private."

"How about one of the recreation rooms?" I asked. "We've got those holographic ones that can simulate all sorts of interesting and exotic and very private locales." And I have unlimited access to the new and not-as-yet-open-to-the-public one, I added to myself.

"Goody. Lead on," she said, hooking her arm into mine.

Well, it didn't take us long to dry off and head in the direction of the new wing of the station. It was still technically under construction, but the workmen had really finished and the power was on; all that remained was to clean up the debris and smooth off the rough spots. I put Carol in

## The Forms of Things Unknown

the rec room looking at the menu of simulations that had already been loaded, and stepped outside to face the confrontation I knew was imminent.

He showed up just as I had foreseen - this annoying young security guard who seemed to have a problem with me. I don't remember his name, but I can't forget his face - he had the kind of sleek, pretty, long-haired good looks that women love and men hate. I guess his appearance annoyed me, but so did his manner. He always said "sir" to me in the most excruciatingly grating manner I can imagine; he somehow managed to make it sound like an insult rather than a title of respect.

"Is there something I can help you with, *sir*?" he asked. It almost made me grind my teeth. "Did the commander know that the safety prohibition is still on in this area?"

"Of course I know it, crewman. I'm here conducting a safety inspection myself," I lied, badly.

"Of course, *sir*," he oozed. "I know you have more important things on your mind," he said, trying to look into the open door behind me, "and thought the orders might have slipped by you."

"Very little slips by me, crewman, but thank you for your concern. Carry on."

"Yes, *sir*!" he said with a salute, then marched away stiffly. The automatic doors had not yet been connected, and he punched a code to open the next hallway entrance. As it closed behind him, I got the powerful flash of an event that has managed to escape my prescience until the very last moment. I quickly stepped up on a wall-fitting to get a glance through the plexsteel window in the door that had just closed, and what I saw shocked even me. The crewman had

# Eight Minute Warning

not taken five steps past the door when an alien jumped out at him.

Now, I'm used to seeing lots of pretty strange-looking creatures in my line of work, so it takes more than an ugly face to startle me. This being, however, had it. It was a vaguely puma-like biped, a full head shorter than the guard but much more powerfully built, in green service coveralls with a huge backpack on. It wasn't its looks that shocked me, though. It was just that I had never seen an apparently sentient creature disembowel an armed guard in less than three seconds before.

The soundproof door kept out even the faintest note of whatever sound he made as he died, so Carol was quite surprised when I ran into the room, grabbed her wrist and said "Come on!"

"Come on? Come where? I thought we..."

"No time! Move!" To her credit, she turned into a good soldier and followed me as quickly as she could. I knew that I would have at least a little warning before the creature leapt on us from behind, but somehow that didn't make me feel any better.

We reached the plaza just seconds before the creature did, and I shoved Carol into the crowd only an instant before the screams of the civilians alerted me to the fact that my playmate had arrived. I spun to face it, unsure of how I was going to defend myself in a bathing suit with no weapons other than my wits, and was rather unnerved to see the creature standing still about seven meters away from me, being hit by half a dozen pulser blasts from the security guards (no doubt alerted when it forced the security door) and emitting a peculiar huffing noise that I just knew was its equivalent of laughter.

After a few seconds it turned and began to unpack its backpack and another rather large box it had apparently carried here while still managing to catch up with me running. It ignored the deadly weapons fire as I would ignore a gentle rain and proceeded to set up some sort of a machine from the parts in the two cases.

The machine was a sort of boothlike affair, and it seemed as impervious to damage as the creature was. The security guards had abandoned energy weapons and were now attempting hand-to-hand, but their best blows simply slid off of it as though they literally were not even hitting it at all. The creature just completely ignored them and went about its business with inhuman speed and certainty, huffing occasionally.

Even though I realized that some kind of portable force-field (more powerful than any I had ever seen, but not impossibly so) would easily account for the creature's shrugging off physical attacks, it was still eerie to watch how completely it ignored them as it went about its task. Even as I ordered an M-ray generator brought, I knew that it was futile. With the certainty my gift allows, I knew that the booth and its protections were examples of a technology not yet developed. The device was the receiver for a time machine, a fact everyone else in the plaza would learn in about four minutes. I didn't need precognition to realize that whatever was going to come through it would be bad news, but I suddenly got a flash that the person most in danger here was...Carol.

Why she should have that dubious honor I wasn't sure, but I didn't waste time trying to figure it out, either. I plunged into the crowd, dragged her through the back of it

# Eight Minute Warning

and hustled her down the corridor to where my designated escape capsule was. On the way, I removed a key from my key ring and pressed it into her hand, saying, "There's enough food in the capsule to take you to the normal patrol lanes - it'll only be a couple of days. When you get back to Earth, this is the key to my house."

"Earth? I'm not going..."

"Shut up and get in," I said as I punched the code that opened the capsule's door. "Whatever is coming through that cabinet is particularly interested in you, don't ask me why. When you get to Earth the infonet will give you my address. Use the key, and when the computer asks who you are tell her you're from the Pussy-of-the-Month Club."

"The *what*?!!"

"Security code. It has to be outlandish enough so my ex won't figure it out. Just sit tight and I'll probably join you there in about three weeks. If I don't show, the house is yours. I love you." With that, I entered the launch code and watched the inner, then outer door close. I couldn't be sure, but I think a little voice squeaked "I love you, too."

By the time I got back to the plaza the creature's task was complete and the cabinet was glowing from within. The glow lasted only a moment, then a being stepped out.

He was almost seven feet tall and the skin that covered about three-quarters of his body was dead white, the white of a glossy enamel paint. The other quarter of his body was done in black and silver, chrome and plexsteel - he was a cyborg, and a mean-looking job at that. There was no reason to have his artificial parts look like that - even in my century, they can make them almost indistinguishable from the

227

## The Forms of Things Unknown

originals. No, this guy was trying to look scary on purpose, and doing a damn good job of it, too.

No sooner was he out of the cabinet than he spoke. As I knew he would, he asked, "Where is Nicholas Kutuzov?"

Backup muscle was already materializing in the cabinet, and I knew it was pointless to try to hide my identity - they would have control of the station in half an hour at this rate. "Here," I said, stepping forward. "But then, you knew that."

The creature was essentially humanoid, but that smile was pure beast. "Ah, Mr. Kutuzov. I've come a long way to meet you. I have need of someone with your rather unusual talents."

"About three hundred years, I'd say. And my talents may be unusual, but they're certainly not unique."

"Three hundred and eighteen years, to be exact. And you do yourself an injustice, Mr. Kutuzov. Many short-range precognitives there may be, but none with your unparalleled record of accuracy. No one in the next three centuries will even approach it, not even your yet-to-be-born progeny."

It was nice to know that I would be remembered for something in the 27th century, even if it was getting me into trouble now. It was also nice to know that I would have children someday. I was almost tempted to ask who the mother would be. Almost. "Even so, time travel seems like an awful lot of trouble to go through just to talk to a dead man who's a really good guesser."

"Humility does not become you, Mr. Kutuzov. In fact, it was not mentioned in your personnel file as a trait you possessed in any degree at all. But I digress. As you must already know, I am here because you can help me to...ah... adjust a few things in my favor."

228

# Eight Minute Warning

"Adjust? You mean you want to change your own history. No deal, pal. Even if I could do something like that, I wouldn't."

"You are most certainly capable of doing what I ask - not on your own, mind you, but I have brought along a little...help. And as for your unwillingness, I have ways to change that."

"If you injure me or try to use neural overrides, my brain will enter a stress state and..."

"I am aware of the biochemical limitations of your precognition, Mr. Kutuzov," he interrupted. "I had no plans to physically or electronically coerce you, but your wife is another matter entirely."

"Your history files are a little off, big guy. I divorced her months ago. She must be four hundred parsecs from here."

"Not your fifth wife, you fool. Your sixth. My records show she arrived at this station this morning."

I couldn't stop the broad grin from spreading across my face, nor could I resist a glance at my watch. It had been exactly seven minutes and sixteen seconds since I had sensed Carol was in danger.

This guy may have been ugly and evil, but he was no dummy. He immediately realized that I had foreseen his plan and flew into a rage - more at himself than at me, I think, but the effect was the same. He got right in my face and shouted, "*Where is she?*!!"

Facing a seven-foot armored cyborg while clad only in swim trunks is not the most comfortable position in the universe, but I knew he didn't dare hurt me even a little for fear of ruining my precognition until the pain faded away,

## The Forms of Things Unknown

and he didn't have that kind of time to waste. "In an escape capsule heading for Earth, far out of range of any of this station's weapons and moving way too fast for any ship to catch up to now."

He regained his composure as quickly as he had lost it. "Very well, my friend," he growled. "I suppose I could not have asked for a better field test of your abilities. Now we'll just have to use some of these innocent bystanders to persuade you."

In the tension of the moment, I had almost forgotten the crowd, but the screams that followed that pronouncement reminded me very quickly. The heavies who had followed Mr. White through the time cabinet were now herding a large number of the civilians into a corner, where they no doubt intended to use them for target practice until I agreed to cooperate.

Amazing as it may seem, though, something else caught my attention a little more, perhaps because my power prompted me to turn around and look at the time cabinet. Some of the invaders were setting up a second cabinet just like the first one, and nearby lay sprawled the apparently dead body of the puma-creature. As I looked, its body seemed to rot away with astonishing rapidity.

"What happened to him?" I asked.

The big cyborg seemed startled that I had turned around to look at the cabinet, apparently ignoring the plight of the others. "Don't you have more important things to worry about? Those people..."

This time it was my turn to interrupt. "Yeah, yeah. Let 'em go. I'll help you. But answer my question."

He seemed a bit wary of my sudden change of heart, but he answered the question anyway while waving to his goons to let the hostages go. "Temporal distortion, Mr.

230

# Eight Minute Warning

Kutuzov. The unfortunate and inevitable side effect of time travel without a receiver. Didn't you wonder how he got here in the first place if he hadn't assembled the receiver yet?"

"The thought had occurred. So your device can be used in two modes, right?"

"Yes. With or without a receiver. But those who travel without a receiver soon end up like poor Epauw."

"And the second receiver?"

"The first one arrived with Epauw. Soon it, too, will cease to function, though machines last longer than organic structures." As he spoke, the last remnants of Epauw dissolved into nothingness. "There, you see? And the first receiver will follow him shortly. The second one, however, came by receiver and so is as permanent as I am."

"So every time you want to time travel, you have to throw away a perfectly good henchman and a brand-new receiver?"

"An unavoidable expenditure, I'm afraid, but well worth it. Shall we talk business now?" he asked, gesturing toward the office area.

"I suppose so," I said, shrugging. "By the way, what's your name? You have the advantage on me."

"I will continue to have that, Mr. Kutuzov," he leered, "but there is no reason you should not know my name, as it will expedite our discussions. I am called Lajard."

"Is that Mr. Lajard, or just Lajard plain?"

"Lajard will do. And now to business," he said, sitting down in my chair behind my own desk. He certainly knew how to gall a person, but I wasn't going to bite. I sat on the sofa.

# The Forms of Things Unknown

"How exactly am I supposed to help you?" I asked. "As you well know, I'm only a short-term pre-see. How am I going to help you with events three centuries from now?"

He grinned that revolting grin again. "You forget, Mr. Kutuzov, that the difference between your power and that of the long-term precognitives is one of kind, not degree. While a standard precognitive's brain receives images directly through time by a process we do not yet understand even in my century, your brain instead follows chains of causality from the present up into the future."

"But the maximum length of those chains is just about eight minutes, less in extremely complex and entropy-laden situations controlled largely by chance. In battles, for instance, my time can drop to as low as forty seconds."

"But your accuracy does not drop. And theoretically, if external variables could be controlled for, your vision could penetrate more than eight minutes."

"That's true, but we're talking about laboratory conditions, and even then I've never broken an hour."

The nasty smile got bigger. "But I have access to laboratory equipment that will not be designed for another three hundred and twelve years," he hissed. "With it, there is no reason you cannot penetrate to my century or even beyond."

I knew he was right, and so did he. Any civilization capable of building a time transmitter could easily build a precognition amplifier; the principle is exactly the same. Whatever device confined the transmission beam to a certain path into the past could easily shield extraneous information from my psychic probe. It would be like removing all wind resistance from a flying object; there might be no limit to how far my mind could tunnel into the future. I don't mind admitting it was just a little bit scary. OK, a lot scary.

# Eight Minute Warning

"When do we start, and what are we looking for?" I asked.

He didn't answer, just smiled even more. I really began to wonder if he would swallow his ears.

It wasn't long before they had set up all sorts of weird equipment, including absolutely nothing recognizable. I take that back. One thing was recognizable - electrodes. Lots and lots of electrodes, taped all over me. It was like the first week at the Center for Psionic Resources, when they were still trying to find out what exactly I could do.

Lajard was leering over me. "It was fortunate you saved us the trouble of having to undress you, Mr. Kutuzov. Time is of the essence, if you'll pardon. Your patrol ships will arrive in a few hours, and even my force fields won't be able to stand up to that kind of massed firepower. Fortunately, we'll be long gone by then." He pointed to a bank of monitors. "Just in case you had any funny ideas about lying about what you see, we'll be watching. We know you can't help but get the images when conditions are right, so there's no point in struggling. My operative," here he pointed to a peach-colored, bald-headed, insectoid fellow sitting behind the console, "will feed your brain the data, and you will be so kind as to image for us. We will record the results, and that will tell us what we have to change. Then we will leave you alone, and two minutes later all of our equipment will self-destruct so as to introduce no unforseen random element into history after we leave. You see? Working for me won't be so bad, after all."

I didn't say anything; I was too busy listening. The little peach bug was quietly complaining to his supervisor that he wasn't being given sufficient time to calibrate his

## The Forms of Things Unknown

instruments and so would have no way of knowing whether the equipment was causing me permanent damage or not. The supervisor was in turn explaining to him in an equally quiet voice that he didn't give a damn if my frontal lobes burned up as long as I gave them the images. Nice guy.

I knew where the little guy was coming from, though. They had made a complete mess of my office in their haste to get set up - crate fragments, tools and other dangerous debris were all over my carpet. A guy could get hurt walking around in there, especially one with bare feet, but since they didn't care if my frontal lobes burned up I guess a punctured foot was no big deal, either. Oh, well, at least the carpet was a dark color and wouldn't show the grease stains.

Anyway, they spent about fifteen minutes running some preliminary tests, and the little bug-guy was nice enough to let me choose my own subjects. Lajard kept going in and out, alternating between watching us and checking the deep-space scanners to make sure the patrols hadn't arrived yet. He also had apparently had words with the station's CO, Commodore Hardy, who was of course being held hostage with the rest of the officers. I had to laugh in spite of the situation - Hardy was a tough old bird who was probably stewing in his own juices right now about being held prisoner on his own station. Even though the alien's firepower and defenses were clearly far superior to ours, he might never recover from the embarrassment.

After what seemed like forever despite my having known about it several minutes before it happened, Lajard walked in and suggested we start. Immediately. I knew the patrol ships had been spotted on the long-range and would be here in less than an hour, but that still gave Lajard all the time he needed.

234

# Eight Minute Warning

Thirty-five minutes and five runs later, Lajard waved goodbye as his men carried out the recording devices and other equipment no doubt too expensive to leave behind. "Don't bother getting up, Mr. Kutuzov," he smirked. "I'm sure your ordeal has worn you out - you look quite pale. If it makes you feel any better, you've made me a very, very rich and powerful man. Goodbye." I could hear his laughter all the way down the hall.

I began removing the electrodes from myself, but waited to head for sickbay until the sounds and smells of self-destructing electronics let me know that they were definitely gone.

"What did you do to your foot?" the doctor scolded as I hobbled into the infirmary a few minutes later. The Commodore was right behind me with about four thousand questions, but the doctor told him that could wait until at least the bleeding was stopped.

"Actually, I can answer you both at once. I stepped on a piece of debris left by the aliens on my office floor. Since they had no time to calibrate the machine, they had no way of knowing I was in excruciating pain, since I wasn't about to tell them and the dark carpet hid the blood."

"Why didn't you tell them you were hurt?" asked the Commodore, but the doctor's grin told me that she had already figured it out.

"Intense pain totally ruins my precognitive capabilities for a while, but since they didn't know I was in pain they didn't know I was just feeding their machine images from my imagination," I explained, wincing as my wound was cleaned.

# The Forms of Things Unknown

"That was brave, but foolish," said the Commodore. "If they had realized you were wounded, they could have had Doc heal you and gone right on, and might not have been so kind to you when they left. Also, what if they realize your images were fake? What's to stop them from coming back another time?"

"Same answer for both questions. They were foolish enough to let me choose my own subjects for the tests and didn't bother to record them - again, they were too pressed for time. I looked forward to see if they would notice the foot trick. An hour was a piece of cake with that machine. Three hundred years was harder, but I was able to find out how to make sure our nasty friend winds up in the custody of his century's authorities. When they implement those changes, they're going to get a big surprise."

The Commodore grinned. "Good work, son. You'll get another promotion out of this for sure, and I'll hate to lose you. But tell me, how did you resist the temptation to look into your own personal future in the time they gave you to practice? I know I couldn't have."

"I couldn't either," I said. "I did take just one little look, a few months into the future. You know Carol McCormac?"

"I think I do," he said. "Very attractive girl."

I smiled as I slid off of the table. "She looks even better in a wedding dress."

236

# About the Author

Maggie McNeill was a librarian in suburban New Orleans, but after an acrimonious divorce economic necessity inspired her to take up sex work; from 1997 to 2006 she worked first as a stripper, then as a call girl and madam. She eventually married her favorite client and retired to a ranch in Oklahoma, but began escorting part-time again in 2010 and full-time again early in 2015 after another divorce (this time amicable). She has been a sex worker rights activist since 2004, and since 2010 has written a daily blog called "The Honest Courtesan" (http://maggiemcneill.wordpress.com/) which examines the realities, myths, history, lore, science, philosophy, art, and every other aspect of prostitution; she also reports sex work news, critiques the way her profession is treated in the media and by governments, and is frequently consulted by academics and journalists as an expert on the subject.

43155054R00137

Made in the USA
Middletown, DE
02 May 2017